SILENCE IS GOLDEN

Silence is Golden

and other stories

Eric Cross

POOLBEG PRESS: DUBLIN

This collection first published 1978 by
Poolbeg Press Ltd.,
Knocksedan House,
Swords, Co. Dublin, Ireland.
© Poolbeg Press Ltd., 1978

The generous assistance of
the Northern Ireland Arts Council and of
An Chomhairle Ealaíon (The Arts Council)
in the publication of this book
is gratefully acknowledged.

Some of these stories were previously published
in various periodicals and broadcast by
Radio Telifís Éireann.

Also published by Poolbeg Press:

Short Stories

The Road to the Shore by Michael McLaverty
A Sexual Relationship by Gillman Noonan
The End of the World by Bryan MacMahon
A Life of Her Own by Maeve Kelly
Yarns by John Jordan
Sixpence in Her Shoe by Maura Treacy
Collected Short Stories by James Plunkett

Plays

The Sanctuary Lamp by Thomas Murphy

Designed by Steven Hope
Cover photograph: Bord Fáilte

Printed by Cahill (1976) Limited,
East Wall Road, Dublin 3.

Contents

The Powder Of Levity

"IT was one of those days in March," said Tim Timothy Tim, " – if I remember rightly it was the twelfth – when, no matter what you'd do, the smoke kept coming down the chimney and into the room so that you couldn't see to hang the kettle."

"At that time," he continued, "I had a hired man, by the name of Aloysius McCafferty Keogh, working for me. He was an orphan leprechaun I'd taken pity on in a weak moment. It wasn't that he was much use about the place but he had a deal of leprechaun's trickery and knowledge which came in useful the odd time."

"Blast it!" said I to him, when my patience was near exhausted, "you'd think that the government, with all their talk of their powers and what they can do, would pass an act of parliament to keep a simple thing like smoke in order and in the right direction."

"They couldn't do it," replied Aloysius, "for they haven't the right understanding of the matter at all. They have only book learning about things like human beings and no knowledge of natural things."

"I couldn't disagree with you less," said I, "but who has the knowledge so?"

"I have it myself," he replied. "'Tis simply a matter of the understanding of opposites. The whole world is nothing but a mixture of opposites. There's day and there's night. There's hot and there's cold. There's man and there's woman. There's not one thing ever that there isn't the opposite to it, rightly seen. And the secret of success in all things is not too much of the one or too little of the other."

"That's a damned fine sermon but the smoke is still

coming down the chimney."

"I'm coming to that, if you'd only have patience. When anything goes wrong the first thing to look for is the two opposites. And what's the matter with that smoke is it has too much of the one and too little of the other. It has too much gravity and not enough of its opposite, levity."

"In spite of all the philosophy, the smoke is still coming down instead of going up. It's all a matter of words with you."

"I've as little regard for words as yourself or, maybe a damned sight less, but thought's the soup before you come to the meat."

With that said he turned to the great chest which he had brought with him as luggage and kept in the cupboard under the stairs. After rooting about in the depths of it for a couple of minutes he came up with a bottle and handed it to me. "There you are," said he. "There's the answer to your problem."

It was a bottle of grey powder, like dust, and round it was a label which read, "The Powder of Levity. Sprinkle carefully, before, after or during meals. Not to be taken lightly".

"Hmmph!" said I, after reading it. "What's the meaning behind the doctor's gibberish?"

"'Tis what we were talking about, if you had any glimmer of understanding at all. 'Tis the answer to the smoke problem. 'Tis bottled levity – the opposite to gravity." With that, he took the bottle from me, uncorked it and peppered a dust of it onto the fire. Before you could think the smoke shot up the chimney as though the bailiffs were after it and we had no more of the bother of it. The day's good deed done, Aloysius put the kettle on for the tea.

The more you thought about it, the more the pity it seemed to have such a useful substance eating its head off in the bottle with laziness and not to be putting it to some good use. We thought and we thought what we might do with it for the good of mankind but with everything we thought there was some fault or other, for, to do right good is one of the most difficult things in the world.

Then happen an election came to the district and two men put up for it – one by the name of Hennigan and the other by the name of Finnegan. Finnegan was the sort of man that anyone in his right senses would vote for, for you couldn't imagine the likes of him being bothered making acts of parliament. He was an easy-going, comfortable class of a man, always ready to let sleeping dogs lie. He'd just strayed into politics by accident and found the seats comfortable and the money aisy.

Hennigan, on the other hand, was the class of man, who, if he was elected would have us all turned inside out and upside down by acts and bye-laws till we were all walking saints with all the fun taken out of living.

We thought the matter over between ourselves at night by the fire and we worked out a great plan, and we had our preparations made.

The night before polling day Hennigan was to have a grand, final rally and speechmaking in the council meeting rooms. The two of us washed and brushed our hair and put on our collars and ties and, after we had the supper taken, off with us to the meeting. It was only half an hour after the meeting was announced to begin so there were very few in the hall. Aloysius, being a very small class of a man, was able unnoticed to slip up to the platform and dust some of the Powder of Levity along the front of the table where they made the speeches.

Soon after closing time the crowd came in to fill up the seats and the performers took up their places on the platform. And a miserable lot they looked too, as though not one of them would be there that night but that he owed Hennigan money and dared not refuse him. Last of all came Hennigan himself, looking just like Hennigan, and there's not much worse could be laid at any man's door than that.

The crowd started to "Hooroo!" and throw things at the platform and enjoy the evening. Then Hennigan came up to the front of the platform and started to make his speech. He was at it for quite a while and was beginning to repeat himself and yet nothing was happening. I was beginning to wonder if perhaps the powder had got damp and the evening would be wasted for us, when, suddenly, "Whoosh!" Hennigan shot up from the platform like a cock pheasant and hit his head a crack on the ceiling.

Though everyone in the audience was surprised there was no one so much surprised as Hennigan himself, as he floated up there, rubbing his head, with his legs dangling and not knowing what could have happened to him. Everyone was gazing up at him with their mouths wide open, thinking it better than anything that they had ever seen in any circus.

"Get me down!" bawled Hennigan. "Get a ladder! Get the police! Get the Fire Brigade!"

Some of the committee rushed out and got a ladder but it wasn't long enough. Then, someone else got a rope and threw one end of it up to Hennigan till he caught it and, when he had a hoult got on it, they hauled him down, hand over fist, like a flag after a celebration. Next, when he was down to earth the chairman poured whiskey into the glass on the table, never minding the water. As soon as Hennigan saw this – and who could blame him – he made a grab for the glass and let go of his hoult on the rope and ... "Whoosh!" away aloft with him again, like a lark to the ceiling. The crowd were delighted with themselves. It was the best political meeting that had been held in the country for many a year.

They threw the rope up to Hennigan again and hauled him down again and they tied the slack of the rope round the leg of the table and Hennigan continued his speechifying, tethered like an ould goat. But all the time the levity was battling with gravity and was gradually

12

overcoming it and the rope could not stand the strain and snapped and off with Hennigan aloft again.

By this time the crowd was really enjoying the evening, calling out "Up Hennigan! Up Hennigan!" as though he was some sort of a jack-in-the-box. It began to look as though we had, perhaps, done more harm to the country than good, for naturally, most people would be only too pleased to vote for a man who had given them such a grand evening's entertainment. And it isn't every politician will obey orders and rise to the ceiling when the crowd shouts "Up Hennigan!"

When they got him down again and tethered him with a stronger bit of rope he only lasted about three minutes when the rope snapped once more and aloft went Hennigan. Well, you should have heard the crowd "Hennigan Abu. Up Hennigan! Hennigan tops the poll!" They hauled him down again and tethered him again, but this time he lasted a minute before he cracked his skull once more on the ceiling. The chairman decided that, after all you can have too much of a good thing, and adjourned the meeting in disorder.

Now the fun was ended the two saddest people in the hall were myself and Aloysius, who had set out to do good and only done harm, for there wasn't a doubt who the people would vote for the next day. But it was our ignorance which made us sad for this wasn't the end of the business by a deal. It was, as you might say, only the beginning. We hadn't made allowances for the fact that all the time Hennigan was performing on the platform the powder of levity was working into the soles of his shoes and was only really getting down to the serious business of the evening.

Hennigan was walking across the hall to the entrance, still with the rope tied to him and one of the committee holding on to it by habit now, as much as anything. When the two of them got to the middle of the hall, some fellow, who had entered into the right spirit of the evening, stepped in and saved the situation. He whipped a knife out of his pocket and cut the rope which tied the two of them together and away shot Hennigan again. But this time he didn't hit the ceiling. The man who cut the rope was a man of brains, all credit to him. In the centre of the ceiling there was a round skylight which they used to slide open on the nights of council meetings to let out the hot air. And your man had judged the cutting of the rope to the nicest thing you ever saw . . . just exactly under the open skylight.

Hennigan shot up through the skylight and to wherever it is in that direction. The crowd assembled outside said that it was as fine a sight as ever they saw in all their born days. The night was bright and clear and they could watch Hennigan, flying away like a rocket, faster and faster, till he was only a speck in the sight of the keenest-eyed man.

He didn't come down for the poll next day and where he was only he himself knew and he sent no address. Finnegan won the election easily and is having a fine, well-paid rest for himself in parliament.

There was a deal of speculation for some time in the locality as to what had happened to Hennigan. Some said that it was due to all the hot air that was in him, while others said that it was some sort of baking powder that his wife used, for she had the name for making a very light cake. We left them to their ignorance.

The schoolmaster, a man of great learning, who knew more about the Hebrides and the rest of the planets than he did about his own doorstep, told those who would listen to him that Hennigan would go in a straight line until he came back to where he started. There weren't many who paid heed to that sort of schoolmaster's learning.

Years passed and Hennigan's wife took a strong notion to get married again and she applied to the court to have the "have his carcase" act put into operation. But the court wouldn't help her for they had no more knowledge of where his carcase was than she had herself.

More time passed and the matter was almost forgotten when, one night at a council meeting in the hall where Hennigan had gone up like a balloon, there were bumpings and scratchings heard under the floor boards and the matter was discussed.

Someone remembered what the schoolmaster had said years before about Hennigan returning to the spot from which he had left but in the opposite direction. Some of them were of the opinion that the scratchings were Hennigan and others were of the opinion that they were due to rats. The two factions went at it hot and heavy. Finally they had to put the matter to the vote. Open up the floor or leave well alone.

The vote came out even and the chairman said that he would not cast his vote at all for he wasn't for setting himself up as Solomon, making judgement between Hennigan and a rat. His considered opinion, he said, was that if it was Hennigan was kicking up the row he would be better able to find his way out than any rat, and, if it was rats, they had enough of them in the meeting already.

The Powers Of Imagination

"YOU'LL remember to give a sop of hay to the cow," said Michael Sullivan, as he drew on his coat.

"Indeed, but I'm less likely to forget that," replied his wife, "than you are to remember the bottle of water from St. Brigid's Well that I've been asking you to get for me for months past."

"Yerra, woman, I'm going on business – not to be traipsing bottles of spring water about the countryside like a mineral-water manufacturer. We've water enough in the well at the door, and as for the rest of it, 'tis all in the power of imagination, as I've told you a hundred times."

"Imagination or no imagination, 'twould be better for you than to be traipsing bottles of poteen round the countryside till one day the guards catch you. 'Tis then you'll want the imagination to pay the fine."

"Guards – where are you? To hear the way you talk anyone would think it was only yesterday I was born. I'd best be off or I'll miss the train."

He started up the track over the shoulder of the hill. The bottle of poteen in his overcoat pocket bumped heavily against his thigh as he walked. It was a pleasant bumping, however, he mused, as soon it would be salved by the pound note he would get from Dick Hegarty for it. Yes, a pound at least.

"A bottle of the best," was the message, "for a man who wants it for greyhounds and won't be mean about the price asked. If he's satisfied, there will be further orders. A strong buyer now, so don't be letting me down and letting yourself down into the bargain."

"A pound a bottle and further orders," Michael Sullivan reflected. "And that might mean, say, a bottle a day. And

16

there were six days in the week, forgetting Sunday, when, most likely, he'd have no need of it for greyhounds. Six days a week at a pound a day. That would be six pounds a week . . . that was a deal better than even a ganger's job with the county council. Six pounds a week . . . and say, fifty working weeks in the year . . . that would be three hundred pounds a year.

"Three hundred pounds a year! What chance had a man to earn that slaving from morning to night, winter and summer, on a mountainy farm? It was every bit as good as a sergeant's job in the guards. And to think of herself bothering him about an ould bottle of well water when he was almost in the way of being set up as a business man. Women were queer . . . they had the bad word for everything and no right use of their imagination at all."

The Kilbrigid train was already in and waiting for the branch-line connection when he reached the station. He took his seat in an empty compartment and cut himself a fill of tobacco and stretched at his ease. Then the foxy-haired fellow came in. He had always a dislike of a foxy man. Somehow they always seemed to spell trouble. The foxy man passed the time of day. Michael packed his pipe and threw open his coat for the matches in his inner pocket before he remembered. But it was too late. The foxy-haired fellow's eyes had spotted the bottle.

"A drop of the right stuff, I suppose," he said, sliding over on the seat. "I hear they have a great reputation for the making of it hereabouts."

But Michael Sullivan was much too quick for him.

"'Tis only a bottle of blessed water I'm taking in to a sick relation," he replied without hesitation.

"Sure — of course it is," replied the foxy man. "Now what would be the price of a right bottle of it," he continued.

"'Tis a bottle of blessed water, I'm telling you."

"Manalive, we're agreed on that. 'Tis the matter of the price and the quality I'm interested in."

17

At that moment, however, the branch-line train pulled in and the foxy-haired man's attention was diverted. He spotted someone he was apparently waiting for down the platform and got hurriedly out of the compartment, and Michael Sullivan was greatly relieved at his going. After all he could be, as likely as not, a guard in plain clothes or a detective, for there was a court in Kilbrigid that day. If only the train would start.

But the momentary relief was cut from its roots when, as the train was on the point of starting, the foxy-haired man jumped into the compartment, this time with two guards, confirming Michael Sullivan's apprehension.

However, they took little notice of him beyond a curt nod to him — or so it seemed. But that was small consolation to him. From somewhere at the back of his mind there came the remembrance that you couldn't be arrested on a moving train. That was why they said nothing and did nothing. They were waiting till he stepped out on to the platform at Kilbrigid. Then they would surround him and arrest him, search his pockets and find the evidence on him.

The group had got into an argument between themselves in the meantime. They were disputing the rights and the wrongs of a case to be heard that day, and it was plain enough from the talk that the foxy-haired man was a detective all right.

"I tell you that he'll get off on a point of law," asserted the detective.

"You're letting your imagination run away with you, young fellow me lad. 'Tis a good thing that you have the guards to protect you from your ignorance," laughed one of the others, who had the stripes of a sergeant. "The law's a trickier thing than you think."

"Will you bet a level pound on it, then?" whipped back the detective.

"I will, I will," replied the sergeant eagerly. "'Twill be the easiest money I ever won."

The matter did not concern Michael Sullivan. He had enough to worry him, but he could not help hearing it. The words and phrases floated into his mind, mingling with his brooding. "A point of the law. . . . The law's a trickier thing. . . ."

Then, suddenly, a ghost of a smile came to his face as an idea blossomed. Guards – where are you! He wasn't born yesterday. The laugh was with him now. Where were they at all? Ah, they had just passed Mauleen. A couple of miles, and they would be coming to the Gorey tunnel . . . the creamery . . . Pat Lucey's cross . . . the main road . . . any moment now.

Suddenly the train plunged into darkness. Sulphurous smoke belched and billowed into the compartment through the wide open window. Quick as a cat he jumped up, whipped the bottle from his pocket and dropped it out and then noisily pulled up the window. When the train came out into the daylight again he was sitting in his corner, quietly smiling to himself. Guards – where are you!

He waited in joyful contemplation of the moment when they had stopped in Kilbrigid and the train had emptied and he was walking away about his business and the sergeant came alongside him and put his hand on his shoulder. Then he would have the laugh on them. But more than that, he would have the law on them. He would show them that they could not do what they liked with Michael Sullivan.

He would let them take him to the barracks through the streets of Kilbrigid. There he would ask for a solicitor. Old Geraghty would be his man. He would claim compensation for unlawful arrest and public loss of character without a shred of evidence against him. He knew the law all right and these fellows could not do just as they liked with law-abiding men. The smile on his face broadened. He had been anticipating a miserable pound for the day. Why, this day would be worth hundreds at

19

least. Michael Sullivan wasn't born yesterday.

The train drew in to Kilbrigid. The sergeant and guard leaped out. Sullivan took his time, drawing his coat round him and buttoning it slowly. He stepped out onto the platform. The foxy-haired detective followed him out. How clever they were – or thought they were with their plan. Just too clever by half. The moment was approaching which would be great retelling through the winter months.

The detective sidled up to him and walked alongside him.

"If it's the right stuff I'll give you fifteen bob for it."

"I don't know what you are talking about," replied Sullivan with great dignity.

"Yerra, man, stop your codding. I've greyhounds myself. I'll make it seventeen-and-six and you can hand it over to me in the waiting-room."

"'Tis a bottle of blessed water, I'm after telling you before."

"All right, all right. Have it your own way. You're a hard man. I'll go to an even pound."

The sergeant and the guard were waiting ahead for him. "Come on, Mick," they called impatiently, "we're late enough already."

The detective drew away. "You'll do no better than that. They are a mean lot in Kilbrigid. An even pound. I'll see you on the 5 o'clock train."

Guards and detectives disappeared into the street and Michael Sullivan was left alone with his empty victory. All that he had done was to make a fool, a double fool of himself. Here he was in Kilbrigid with the whole day wasted before him, empty of purpose, devoid of profit, just because he had let his imagination run away with him.

He dared not show his face into Hegarty's now unless he wanted dog's abuse. He wandered round the town looking into the shop windows. He had a pint and a bite to eat in a pub. He walked out one road and then another in order to fill the empty, mocking hours. He had another drink and got an empty wine bottle from the barman and then went along to St. Brigid's Well outside the town and filled it. He might as well be doing that as anything.

He took his seat in the return train early. As 5 o'clock approached it began to fill. The sergeant and guard got into the compartment, but, beyond a nod, paid no attention to him. Just before the train started the detective came bustling along, looking for them, and came breezily in.

"Come along, sergeant, pay up and look smiling. You can't pull wool over the eyes of the detective force, you know."

"All right, all right, me boy. There's your pound for you. But don't let it go to your head. 'Tis but beginner's luck – and you'll probably pay dearly for it."

The detective took the pound and kissed it in triumph. The train started, and after a few moments he slid over to Michael Sullivan. Nodding towards the bulge in his overcoat pocket he said: "I see you didn't do your bit of business. I told you that they were a mean lot in Kilbrigid. But I won't go back on my offer. A pound and it's a deal."

Michael Sullivan wasn't in the mood for reviving the subject, with all its bitter personal recriminations, and answered him snappishly.

"I'm telling you that it's a bottle of blessed water. The relation was taken away to the hospital and I was too late." But even as he said the words, almost mechanically, there was a stirring in his mind. It wasn't quite clear yet, but some sort of an idea was being born.

"Well – they're tough, mighty tough in the West. Come on, man, make it a deal for twenty-two-and-six."

Michael Sullivan held his peace. He was letting the idea dry its wings.

"All right – 'tis as you say. 'Tis a bottle of blessed water, and I'm paying twenty-two-and-six for it. Now, will that do you? I'll pay you over the money now and you can leave the bottle on the seat when you get out."

The idea was taking form, though it was not yet quite distinct. "I wouldn't have it on my conscience to be swindling any man or to be selling him a thing under false pretences. 'Tis but a bottle of blessed water. Let the sergeant there judge."

With that he drew the bottle from his pocket and handed it to the sergeant. The sergeant scanned it carefully. He drew the cork and smelt the contents of the bottle with leisurely deliberation. He put the bottle to his lips and tasted it, rolling it round his mouth. Then he smacked his lips, rammed the cork back tightly into the bottle and handed it back to Sullivan.

"'Tis the true, genuine and unadulterated article – and well I should know it, being brought up on it almost, as you might say. Time and time again it has saved my life. 'Tis a certain cure for rheumatism, sciatica and pains in the bones." And as he made this solemn pronouncement he winked very, very slowly and solemnly.

The detective returned to the bargaining. "Well – it's a deal, then. I'm satisfied."

But events took a quick turn. The sergeant had done a bit of quick thinking and before Michael Sullivan replied he chipped in.

"'Tis the sort of thing that a man wouldn't care to be putting a price on or valuing in money, but I am just thinking that there is nothing in this world would please my missus more than for me to bring her home such a bottle after my visit to Kilbrigid. Her mother always has the sciaticy bad in the winter and she'll be visiting her next week. I'll go to twenty-five bob for it."

"For a bottle of water from a well?"

"Sure we know that. Haven't I tasted it myself? What else would it be or would I be buying?"

The next station was Michael Sullivan's. He drew the coat round him and started to button it.

"Twenty-seven-and-six," said the detective.

"Twenty-eight-and-six," chipped in the sergeant.

"Twenty-nine shillings," added the detective.

"Twenty-nine-and-six," spoke up the sergeant. "I wouldn't be spoiling a good thought for a miserable shilling or so."

The train drew into the station. Michael Sullivan got up from his seat.

"Here, take the two notes," said the detective, proffering him thirty shillings. Michael Sullivan undid his coat and drew out the bottle. He got the two notes into his fist and handed over the bottle to the detective. "Ye're witnesses, every man of you, that 'tis a bottle of blessed water I'm selling."

"We are, we are," the company chorused. "I suppose that it's his lucky day," added the sergeant with a private wink to Sullivan. "And no man can be beat when the luck runs with him. 'Tis better to be born lucky, I suppose, than to be born intelligent. Good night to you now."

"It's a queer thing after all," Michael Sullivan thought, as he climbed up the dark mountain track, with the two notes held sweetly in his fingers, "'tis a queer thing all right, what a power there is in the imagination: that a man should go against the hearing of his own ears and the sense of his own reason because of it. And to think that that is the sort of fellows we have running the country for us and that's the sort of fellows herself is warning me against. Guards — where are you!"

"Well, I suppose after all your day's traipsing about the countryside you forgot the bottle of water for me," was his wife's greeting as he entered the kitchen.

"I tell you, woman, that I was on business bent and I had no time to be worrying myself about bottles of water."

"The tea is by the fire for you. Wisha! I don't suppose that you'll get sense till the guards catch you and charge you dearly for the teaching of you."

"Guards, me eye!" Michael Sullivan laughed. "To hear the talk by you one would think that I was only born yesterday. Guards teach me, indeed! 'Tis the clever guard will be the match for Michael Sullivan — or detective either."

Frank Of The Frogs

YOU have probably seen him yourself on the roads of Ireland, on his aimless circuit. One of those Ishmaels of the roads – the "travelling men" – wandering alone, wrapped in their rags, shrouded in their own strange thoughts. The fantasies which isolate them from the rest of society are hinted at in the names by which they come to be known at their regular posts of call – Donovan the Doctor, Paddy of the Bush, The Munster Fusilier, The Strong Man, and – Frank of the Frogs.

From the rest of them, Frank of the Frogs is distinguished by the steel tipped lance which he carries, on which is usually impaled the carcase of a frog. Other than this there is little strange about him beyond the strangeness common to his class. It is only at the sight of a frog that the fire of the frenzy which smoulders within him bursts into a blaze and changes him into a gibbering monomaniac – into Frank of the Frogs.

But this particular Frank of the Frogs is not the first man who has borne the odd title. He is not the first man even of his own family who bore the title, for it was the name of his grandfather before him. But of *him*, men used the title with a measure of awe and respect and not with a jesting pity.

Frank MacAuliffe, the original Frank of the Frogs, was a small, mountainy farmer. Beyond good health and a steady head he had little but the grass of three cows and a few sheep on the common mountain side. One day, while opening a gap in a wall, he came across the dried carcase – as sometimes you may in a dry wall – of a frog which had died while in hibernation. It was a curious thing and an event in the dull round of the day worth the telling and

25

the showing at the scoroiucht, when the day's work was done. He put it into the tin tobacco box which he carried and turned back to his work.

That night, at Dan Micky's, he pulled out his box and showed his find, for the wonder of all. This one had heard tell of such a thing; another remembered, as a lad, having seen the like before. Someone else wondered how it had come to be at all. The novelty of the find was almost exhausted when, from the chimney corner, Mike Kelleher spoke up after a long gazing at the shrivelled carcase.

"'Tis a curious thing, alright," said he. "But it is more than that. It is a sign and a token, for it was ever said amongst the old people, that the finding of such a thing is a great fortune to the man who finds it. It was handed down by them, in the old wisdom which is dying out of the world, that there's wealth in the land where a man finds frogs. Keep it by you, Frank, for though sometimes the old people spoke in riddles, 'tis they who knew."

The nightly scoroiucht broke up. Each man went his own way home, with the echoes of the night's talk as company along the lonely paths. For a while Frank MacAuliffe lay awake, his thoughts browsing over the pregnant saying, "There's wealth in the land where a man finds frogs."

With the morning he awoke to the immediate urgencies of the day before him. Once or twice, during an idle moment of the day, the previous night's wonderings returned to him with their lure and their mystery. "Wealth in the land" – whatever way you looked at it it was a comforting thought, without evil in it, for a man to have at the back of his mind. Meanwhile there was a rock to be fired and split for the making of a new bit of a field. There was a patch of near bog to be drained and added to another field. He found a piece of lamb's wool and bedded his curiosity in it in the tin box. That night he put the box into a seldom opened drawer so that he would not lose it.

Pishogue, oracle or the mere mundane result of industry, from that day of the finding of the frog, everything that Frank MacAuliffe put his hand to prospered. He bought when prices were low and he sold always when they were at their highest. Neither crops nor cattle nor weather ever seemed to go against him but always with him. He became the envy and the pride of his neighbours. They came to know him no longer as Frank MacAuliffe, but as "Frank of the Frogs" – the man of good fortune.

Mike Kelleher died and much of the old lore died with him. The younger generation neither cared nor knew how MacAuliffe came to get his nickname.

By the time that MacAuliffe himself came to die he had fortuned two daughters well; he had settled one son on a well stocked farm and he had extended his own farm to the grass of twenty cows with three hundred sheep on the mountain.

Joe Frank, the married son at home, took over the prosperous place. If he did it no good, to give him his due, he did it no harm but nursed it in contentment until, in turn, he handed it over, to his son son, Frank, who took over the routine of the place.

Then one day, while he was opening up a long choked drain, he came across a clamper of hibernating frogs. At the sight of them he drew back and leaned on his spade. "Frogs." Frogs! There was that story about his grandfather, which he had heard as a child, about frogs. It had something to do with the luck and the prosperity which he had so that he was known as "Frank of the Frogs". It was only an old story. He cut short his musing and carried on with his work till the day was done.

After his supper, he went down the road to Batt Hurley's, for a piece of the night as usual and, in the course of the night's talk, he added the incident of his strange finding to the day's news. The story of his grandfather was recalled, as well as could be remembered.

The memories of the older men stirred and each threw in his remembered scrap. "Frogs, eh. There was a saying amongst the people of bygone generations that frogs and luck went hand in hand. . . . Yes, I remember to hear my father speak of that. Where you find frogs there is wealth in the land. Frogs. Frank of the Frogs." By degrees the subject was worn away and gave place to some other topic.

But when Frank MacAuliffe walked home alone that night the snippets of talk still echoed in his ears. "Where you find frogs, there also you will find wealth. . . . Frogs and luck go together." Yerra, that was all old nonsense. And yet . . . . you never know. The old people did have a curious wisdom and knowledge of their own.

The night's sleep swept his thoughts clear of the notion and it was not until he caught sight of the drain on which he had been working the previous day that the thoughts returned to him. "Wealth . . . to find wealth. That were better than to be a slave, from dawn to dark, of land and animals and weather. Yerra, it was all ould cod. The world wasn't run on those lines." He spat on his hands and took a firm grip on his spade and got on with the job. But again and again that day, and the following days, his idle thoughts returned to and dallied with the suggestive idea. "Wealth in the land where you find frogs. . . . Wealth. . . . To travel the world and to see its wonders. . . . To wear fine clothes. . . ." Again and again he hurled such foolish thoughts from his mind and immersed himself in his work. "What foolishness to be paying heed to the talk of some old woman in the chimney corner . . . the old pishogues which the ignorant people of those times mistook for wisdom. . . . To blazes with such nonsense!"

But in a lull in his work, in a back-easing pause, the thought returned in all sorts of guises "People had found wealth buried in the land. There was no denying that." Not so very long ago he had read a bit in the paper which told how a man, ploughing, had struck the ploughshare into a chest of sovereigns. It had happened once. It could happen again.

He remembered the briar-covered liss in the bottom field and the talk he had heard of it as a child. "Who made it? Why did they make it? What was inside it? The fairies, me eye . . . but someone had made it and made it for a good reason."

For weeks he scrupulously avoided the liss and put any intruding thought about it from his mind, yet he found himself turning a half buried stone in a field or exploring a hole in a wall for no good reason. But there was nothing there. There was never anything there. Why should there be? If there was anything to be discovered, if there was wealth hidden, it was in the liss. . . . The wealth betokened to his grandfather and now to him by the frogs.

The day inevitably came when he took a spade and crowbar and went down alone to the liss. After many hours of labour he succeeded in levering away the stone which sealed the entrance to it and squeezed his way into the low chamber which it had blocked. By the dim, flickering light of a candle he explored every corner of the cavity — and found nothing. The next day he returned, with better light, and all day long, without ceasing for food or drink, he searched, lifting the flagstones of the floor, tearing down the walls, but still he found nothing. By the end of a week he had torn the liss asunder and levelled it to the ground and knew for certain that it contained nothing.

The treasure of the frogs was not there. But the liss was not all the land. It was only a small part of the land for which twice the frogs had indicated that it contained wealth.

The daily work of the farm was forgotten as he tore down walls and ditches, prised over rocks and delved in drains and uprooted trees. The cattle were neglected and sickened. There was no ploughing done, no crops sown. From dawn to dark Frank MacAuliffe delved and dug with an ever increasing urgency as the treasure still evaded him. In the middle of the night, spurred by some haphazard inspiration of his fevered mind, he would light a lantern and hurry out with his spade.

The neighbours, meeting him on the road, looked at him askance. He no longer heeded them. Between themselves they began to pity and to fear him. They referred to him, amongst themselves, as Frank, Frank of the Frogs.

He paid no heed to them, in either their pity or their fear. The mania which now possessed him rode him savagely and ruthlessly to destruction. Slowly at first, but with ever increasing pace, the prosperity which he had inherited was dissipated. Cattle and sheep were sold for a song. What matter, compared with the treasure of the frogs?

The end came and the land which he had rooted and torn asunder and laid waste passed from his name and his control. There was nothing left after the sale but a few pounds for the anodyne and the illumination of drink. That finished, he took to the roads and the mission of vengeance which had been revealed to him – and which dominates his life – the extermination of all traces of the laughing, deceiving frogs which had tricked him, robbed him and beggared him.

Mr. Dunphy's Phenomenon

MR. DUNPHY remembered quite distinctly the onset of what he came to call the phenomenon. It occurred on January the eleventh – the day on which the Bank Rate was raised by one per cent. Not, of course, that the two events were related in any way except by the coincidence of date.

He had switched out the bedroom light and was in the act of swinging into bed, having kicked off his slippers, when his eye caught a flicker of light in the mirror on his dressing table. Odd, he thought. The thick curtains were closely drawn across the window. There was little chance of a passing flash from outside penetrating them. It was possibly a touch of indigestion affecting his eyes. He got into bed and, with the easy mind of a well ordered life, was asleep within a few minutes without giving the incident any further thought.

But, the following night the incident was repeated. Now, above all things, Mr. Dunphy had by nature a neat and tidy attitude towards life. It was this aspect of his character which had, most probably, drawn him into the law and it was, as the confidential clerk to Messrs. Clutter, Clutter and Clutter, that this fundamental character had, over the years, been consolidated. His function in life was the preservation and maintenance of established order; in his vocation to maintain the scales of Justice in equilibrium; in his personal life, to accept the laws of the state, of the church and the conventions of society. Untidiness, whether in a material or a mental sense, was an affront to him. The unexplained, the unaccounted for, disturbed him. Such had no place in his well considered routine where everything had a place and everything was in its place. So, he was not a prey to surprise or alarm. His experience had shown him that, with patience and time, the unexpected would always yield to reason and a rational interpretation and subside into the matter-of-fact order of life.

So it was that, on the repetition of the incident, he approached it with the calm objectiveness of a scientist faced with an apparent anomaly in a fundamental law. To use a phrase which he himself would not have used no matter how appropriate – he kept his cool.

He went over to the window and examined the hang of the curtains carefully and made absolutely certain that no chink of light from outside could possibly penetrate them. He returned to the edge of his bed and sat down. The faint light was still apparent in the mirror. He proceeded to the next stage of his investigation and rocked to and fro on the bed. The ghostly glow moved in unison with his movements. Next, he confined his movement to his head. Again the light coincided with his movement. He then put his hand up to his head. The light was obscured. He removed his hand. The dim glow returned. He repeated the series of experiments, confirming his previous results. The light was, in some way, intimately connected with himself. It was located in or about his head. The complete seal of the curtains and the absence of any other form of light in the room ruled out the possibility of a reflection from the shining surface of his bald pate.

There was nothing that he could do about the matter in the immediate circumstance of time and space. It was a rule of his life never to bite off more than he could chew. His training in the process of the law assured him of the wisdom of hastening slowly. Eight hours of solid and unperturbed sleep was an essential factor in his pattern of life. He got into bed.

The following morning, while shaving, the mirror showed nothing untoward. But then, of course, the electric light was on. Having finished his toilet he made the experiment of switching the light off and viewing his reflection again in the mirror. In the darkness of a January morning the luminescence was immediately apparent. Faintly, it was true, but, equally truly, apparent. The phenomenon could not be accounted for as a delusion of the night, the hallucination of indigestion or a tired brain.

For the next few days, particularly in the mornings and at his bedtime, he methodically examined the phenomenon. In the evenings after his meal, sitting before the fire with his post-prandial pipe, he sought possible explanations for it. He remembered an article which he had read in "The Reader's Digest" on Bioluminescence. The copy was handy on his bookshelf but on re-reading it he gained little enlightenment. Nor did he gain much from another article on "Waves of the Brain" in the same time-saving *vade mecum*. He remembered stories of an eerie glow produced by decaying fish. He recalled, years ago, seeing the phosphorescence on the sea on a summer's night. He considered the glowworm and the firefly and consulted articles on both these in the Britannica but the explanations offered seemed to be in no way apposite to his own case.

Unable, for the moment, to explain the phenomenon, he turned his attention to what possible effect and interference it might have upon the details of his daily life, should it persist. Fortunately, the windows of his office were so obscured that even in the height of a summer's day it was always necessary to have the lights switched on fully. But his life was not wholly confined to the office. There were frequent occasions when he had to be present in court or to lunch with clients or counsel. Though, as he had proved, wearing a bowler hat would definitely obscure the light, he could hardly wear one on such occasions. Though it would hide the light it would, at the same time, draw attention to himself. Even if he pleaded a disfigurement for such eccentricity, apart from being a direct lie, the end result would be the same – a drawing of

33

attention to himself, which was a denial of his whole nature. Nor could he contemplate attending Mass on Sunday or playing his weekly round of golf while wearing a bowler.

These were, however, the comparatively leisured and unhurried considerations of possible eventualities and predicaments. More urgent and practical consideration became necessary when he noticed, as the days passed, that the phenomenon was quite rapidly losing its original faint and diffused character. Slowly, but undeniably, it was concentrating and taking on the definite form of a circlet suspended an inch or so above the crown of his head. At the same time its brilliance increased. Though still unnoticeable in strong electric light or open sunlight it was becoming easily apparent in the morning light of the bathroom.

Already he had noticed a curious look in the eyes of his sister who kept house for him. Fortunately she was very short sighted and, for the time at least, he could brush aside any comment from her as the result of that.

A man not trained in the impassive impersonality of the law might, in such circumstances, have panicked. Not so Mr. Dunphy. Sitting before the fire with his pipe and evening tot of whiskey, he viewed the matter objectively as he would view the predicament of a client. He envisaged the possibility of having to live with the phenomenon for the rest of his life. He envisaged the complete disturbance which it was bound to create in the even tenor of his life, destroying the equilibrium which it had taken him years to achieve and disrupting the successful habits of a lifetime. He was, at present, the captain of his soul and the master of his fate. That would be taken away from him.

The phenomenon, if it progressed at its present rate, must inevitably reach a state where he could no longer conceal it. Then attention would be focussed upon him in the most blatant and vulgar form. He would be hounded and pursued by publicity. Even though this public attention should prove to be but a nine days' wonder, the harm which it would do to his life would be irreparable.

The longer he considered the matter the more he realised that he was trapped and that there was nothing that he could do about it. Similar situations – an impasse, a roundabout of futile thinking – did arise occasionally in the course of his work. He had found, in experience, that the sterile circling of thought could often be successfully broken by consultation with an outside mind, preferably with someone having pertinent knowledge about some detail of the impasse. It was often the simple fact of the discussion alone which succeeded, as though akin to the opening of a window and letting in fresh air upon a stifling atmosphere.

But to do that, in this particular case, would merely be to accelerate the position which he feared. In any case who was there whom he could consult in this way? His doctor would be of no use. Science, which could not explain a mere firefly's luminosity, was useless. Furthermore he knew no scientist.

There was, of course, the Church. That at least had some academic or historical acquaintance with phenomena somewhat similar to the matter of concern but he viewed broaching the subject in that particular direction with reluctance.

He considered himself to be, without question, a loyal member of the Church, paying his dues generously and promptly by banker's order, fulfilling meticulously the annual duties expected of him and accepting the teaching of the Church with an equal faith to that with which he accepted the established law of the land. The arrangement was satisfactory, locking in with the rest of his life. To put his predicament before the Church would most certainly destroy this arrangement, for the Church would see the matter wholly from the point of view of its own vested interest and ignore *his* vested interest.

No. He was trapped. There was no possible way out. Then, out of the blue, illumination came to him. Though the Church offered the greatest potential danger to his future peace, at the same time it offered – if unburdening himself might help to ease the situation – a means to this without publicity. It offered the inviolate secrecy of the confessional.

In the matter of ways and means, he considered the local clergy. His knowledge of them, directly, was slight enough, but by way of his sister, whose whole life revolved round the affairs of the parish and the clergy, it was very extensive, provided that it was inverted from her evaluation. He recalled that she had a very low opinion of the senior curate, wondering were he a priest at all, so little was he concerned beyond the bare minimum of his duties. That, in Mr. Dunphy's interpretation, was high recommendation.

Before the illumination was dulled by possible traitor thoughts he picked up the phone and contacted Father Ryan, asking for a few minutes of his time the following evening to discuss a personal problem. Father Ryan, knowing Mr. Dunphy's substantial reputation, readily agreed.

* * * * *

Father Ryan opened the door himself. He took Mr. Dunphy's hat and ushered him into the sitting room. Both hall and sitting room were brilliantly lit. He proferred Mr. Dunphy one of the two armchairs. They discussed the weather and the political situation for a few minutes.

"Now, Mr. Dunphy, this little matter which you would like to discuss with me?"

"I am coming to you, Father, for counsel's opinion, one might say; for expert advice on a matter which is a little out of my range. I can assure you that it in no way concerns either the law of the land or the law of the Church but, as the matter is a very personal matter and though it is not exactly a matter of confession, I would be pleased if you would treat it with the discretion of the Church as a matter of confession and allow me the privilege of the secrecy of confession."

"I am sure, Mr. Dunphy, knowing you as a member of the parish and your professional reputation, that that can be granted. Now, what is it?"

Mr. Dunphy paused for a moment. "If I attempt to tell you in words, Father, you will, with justification, immediately think that I have taken leave of my senses or that I am insane or that I am simply seeking to make a fool of you. I simply could not expect you to believe me. It is a case where seeing is believing. May I ask you to make a simple experiment? Would you mind switching off the light for one moment?"

Father Ryan got up from his chair and went over to the door to fulfil the somewhat odd request. The room was plunged into darkness. There was a moment's silence, then Father Ryan exclaimed "Good Heavens, Mr. Dunphy. Can I believe my eyes?"

"Yes, Father, you can. Come closer and exmine it."

The priest came to Mr. Dunphy's chair and, wide eyed and open mouthed, examined the phenomenon at close range. There was again a silence between the two men. Then Father Ryan resumed his seat.

"That, Father, is the matter which I would like to discuss with you and about which you might be able to advise me."

Mr. Dunphy then told the priest his story from the beginning. Then he put the phenomenon into the context of his life, pointing out all the possible effects which it was likely to have. Father Ryan listened with rapt attention, while all the time his eyes remained fascinated by the top of Mr. Dunphy's head.

"So you see, Father, the predicament in which I find myself," concluded Mr. Dunphy.

"I do. I most certainly do," the priest concurred.

Again there was a period of silence between them. The priest gazed into the fire, now and again raising his head to glance at Mr. Dunphy's head in order to convince himself that he was not dreaming. He asked one or two questions which Mr. Dunphy answered.

"I am sure, Mr. Dunphy, that out of your professional experience you will realise that it would be quite impossible for me to advise you on such an extraordinary matter as this immediately and out of hand. It is quite out of the range of my experience. I would have to give it considerable thought and attention. Could you give me a day or two at least? You may rest fully assured that what I have seen and what you have told me will not go beyond ourselves."

Mr. Dunphy naturally agreed. The two men returned for a few minutes to the everyday world and then Mr. Dunphy took his leave, satisfied with the airing, as it might be called, and satisfied with his choice of Father Ryan.

Father Ryan returned to his chair and sat for a long time digesting his most unusual experience. Mr. Dunphy, either by acumen or luck, had chosen his confidant well. Father Ryan was a man of like nature. He, too, had contrived and achieved a well ordered and even way of life. He had shielded it, as well as he could, against undue disturbance, interference and untoward predicaments. In so doing he had developed a definite distaste for the handling of hot potatoes. Mr. Dunphy could be absolutely certain that what had been seen and what had been said that evening would remain inviolate.

Then, turning his thoughts to Mr. Dunphy himself, he knew that he could not advise him and furthermore, even if he could, would not do so. At least, not directly. After long years in the confessional and all that he had learned there of human nature and the workings of the human mind, he knew that Mr. Dunphy's thoughts lay deeper than his expression. They were, as he remembered from his studies in natural philosophy, in the amorphous stage. They needed just a speck of dust on which to crystallise — a hint, just a suggestion. No more. That would rescue them both. Two days later he wrote to Mr. Dunphy a very carefully composed letter, fully conscious of the fact that Mr. Dunphy, with his legal training, was well schooled in reading between lines.

"Dear Mr. Dunphy,

I have given the matter of our discussion the other evening my very long and earnest consideration.

Though the "phenomenon", as you call it, seldom, if ever, occurs nowadays, according to ecclesiastical history and tradition, in the early days of the Church it was not an altogether unusual occurrence. It was then recognised and attributed to be the product and the outward sign of a wholly sinless or blameless life.

I am sure that you will realise that, as a simple humdrum working secular priest, I have little, either in my parish experience or in my education, on which to advise you about your course of possible action in this matter. I am, as it were, but an articled clerk compared with a long established senior counsel in such a matter.

You could, if you require it, get much more detailed and expert advice from a member of the Jesuit community. They have the requisite academic training in the refinements of interpretation of the moral law and of matters of conscience in relation to individual and particular cases such as yours is. There is a Father Osmium who has a very high reputation in this respect.

But, in the end, as I am sure that you yourself understand, the decision as to what you should do rests wholly with yourself and your conscience. The doctors — even the Jesuits — may advise but in the end the cure is brought about by the patient himself.

"Verbum satis sapienti."

Rest assured that, as far as I am concerned, our conversation remains between ourselves alone. As a priest you have my prayers. As a man you have my sympathy and understanding.

Yours very sincerely,
T. Ryan.

Mr. Dunphy read the letter through slowly and carefully. He read it again, this time paying more particular attention to that which lay between the lines. The requisite breath of fresh air seeped into his thoughts. The amorphous thoughts which had been at the back of his mind were precipitated and crystallised. He was of the "sapienti", and could recognise both a wink and a nod.

That day he arranged with the last of the Clutters to take part of his annual holidays at the end of the week. He arranged the work of the office accordingly. He informed his sister that he would be away for a few days, packed his travelling bag and, at the end of the week, departed.

He returned a week later. Where he had been and what he had done was his own business. That evening, breaking his usual annual routine, he went to confession. For the first time in his life he went to the Jesuits who had "the requisite academic training in the refinements of interpretation in the moral law and of matters of conscience in relation to individual and particular cases."

On the way to Mass on Sunday he met Father Ryan. Not alone out of courtesy, he raised his hat. In fact he raised it just a fraction higher than was the normal custom. "Verbum satis sapienti" can be expressed in a gesture as well as words.

The Grey Rat

THE place is known as Ballygerrat – the townland of the Gerrats. But that isn't the rights of it at all. Time changes names as it changes everything else, for time is change.

If you look up at the shield carved on the archway going into the demesne you can still see the faint outline of a small beast. It is hard to make out exactly what it is now, for time and the weather have worked on the stone too. But in living memory the figure could be seen to be that of a rat – a grey rat – and that is what the name was a long time back – the name of the people and the place, Grey Rat and Ballygreyrat.

The people have gone. Soon the place will be taken over by the government or by strangers. The archway will be pulled down and with it the grey rat will vanish and be lost. It will all only live on in the story and that maybe not for long, for the people nowadays have lost the interest in the old stories and the respect for the meaning and the mystery and the wisdom behind them.

It used to be told that it was because of a grey rat that the family came to fortune and to fame. Whatever they were in the beginning, whatever their names may have been, one of them, one day, came across a hole in a bank of a ditch and as he watched he saw a grey rat come out carrying a gold coin in its mouth. The rat went back and, as though it was clearing for a nest for itself, it brought out another gold coin and then another and another. The unknown man went off and got a spade and returned and opened up the hole which the rat had made into the bank and there he came across a fortune in gold and treasure.

That was the beginning of the family. Whatever their name may have been they became the "grey rats" and, as time did its work, the name became "Gerrat". But the family never forgot the grey rat. The grey rat never forgot the family. Whenever one of them was about to die a grey rat would be seen about the house, be the death at home or abroad. The reason for that no man can tell, but then we don't know everything, and it may be that the knowledge which we have is still not the most important.

That happened a long time ago and many generations back. The Gerrats prospered in fortune and in fame. They built the big house. They built the wall around the demesne. Ballygerrat grew up at the gate with tradesmen, craftsmen, workshops and houses for the people employed by the Gerrats and supplying the Gerrats. It rose with them. It shared their fullness and it suffered their fall.

Time that eats away stone, changes names, eats away also at families and their fortunes. Time and the two wars ate into the family. Taxation and the changed values ate into their fortune.

In the end there was only Miss Amelia left of them all, and she grew old and things went hard with her. One by one she sold the pictures off the walls. Then the silverware and the furniture had to go. Rooms were emptied of their contents and their grandeur and the doors were locked on their emptiness. The only servants left were old Biddy and Sam who were almost as old as herself and as much a part of the place as herself. With the blind courage of pride they fought a rearguard action against the inevitable. They botched, they mended, they made do.

Every Thursday Sam would tackle up the old pony to the tub trap and drive Miss Amelia the half mile down the drive to the town to do the week's shopping. They would stop at Frank Cassidy's. Old Frank would come out, as in the old days, to take the orders that in former times had made Cassidys. Two pounds of sugar, half a pound of tea, a stone of flour. Miss Amelia would take the few shillings out of her bead purse. Then on to Burke, the butcher, and the same performance for a couple of pounds of neck of mutton.

To anyone who did not know it looked like a child's game, a playacting. Miss Amelia dressed in clothes which you would see only in old magazines and acting with a style which has long gone from the world. To anyone who did not know it was laughable. To those who did know it was still laughable but with that laughter which is a staunch for tears.

The weekly visit ended, Sam would jolt the tottering old pony up with a shake of the reins. Miss Amelia would nod her head in acknowledgment of the passers-by, and they would return under the archway and up the drive to the cold and empty shell of a house and to dreams and to courage for another week.

It is in the nature of things that when one thing goes up another goes down. It is also in the nature of things that slow rise brings slow fall and quick rise, quick fall.

While the Gerrats sank outside the town there was a man rising. He started with a garage. He went on to tractor ploughing and harvesting. He bought wool. Everything he touched seemed to turn to success. He grew wealthy and he got an idea of himself.

Ballygerrat, like the Gerrats, was sinking down. John Blake, for that was his name, moved in with his money and his idea of himself. He forced the sale of the Hotel. He put up a modern store and, with his money, could buy cheaply, and in the beginning sell cheaply. Frank Cassidy had to put up the shutters for the last time. They might call his successor grabber and gombeen but times were hard and they were forced to take his goods and the employment he gave.

His little success went to his head. For to measure success against Ballygerrat which was dying and feeble, was not a great comparison. Only to a small man was it so much of a success. He boasted that he was a different man – a man who made the future – and that was a bold thing for anyone to say. It was a thing that only a man without wisdom and without tradition would dare to say.

The next step in his planning was to become the owner of the Gerrat house and the Gerrat lands and the reflected glory of the Gerrats. He even hinted that he already had architects' plans drawn for the reconstruction of the house when, soon, it would pass out of the hands of the last of the Gerrats.

In the meantime he acted as though all this was a certainty and only a month or two or a year or two divided him from his ambition. Without leave or the asking, he would walk round the place and in his eye measure it up. He walked the fields and laid his plans for their future. He eyed the woods and estimated the price he would get for the timber when he cut them down. Miss Amelia was unaware of his existence. He laughed at old Sam's objection to his intrusion.

Miss Amelia was taken ill. Her age and her scant diet were hindrances to her courage and she weakened and had to take to the bed. It was but good news to John Blake – the man who made the future. Each day now he wandered through the grounds of the Gerrats. Each day he expected would be for almost the last time before it was his.

On one such of his visits he was poking round amidst the stables and outbuildings, working out this and estimating that, when an old grey rat came out of a hole in the wall. Old and feeble and weak, it was a suitable target for his strength and he slashed at it with the ashplant which he carried. The rat retreated into a corner, wounded. John Blake slashed at it again. The rat, summoning up the last of its strength, leapt at his hand and sank its teeth deeply into his wrist. Blake, with a wince of pain, shook it off and crushed it with his heel. He did not see or heed Biddy, going from window to window, drawing the curtains in broad daylight.

He ran the half mile down the drive to the doctor but the doctor was out on a call and no one knew where he was. Blake went to the chemist who washed the wound and did what he could for it. By the time the doctor returned from helping Sam and Biddy with the decencies of death it was too late for him to do anything for Blake. The poison of the rat was well established in his bloodstream. In the arrogant self assurance of his inviolability he refused to go to hospital but went to bed in the hotel which he now owned.

The following day he was in a high fever. The day after that the town fell silent. Through his delirium he could hear the tolling of a bell. Soon afterwards he heard the shuffling of feet, the feet of everyone of the town as they followed the coffin of Miss Amelia to the family grave and with her body buried their own roots, their own beginnings.

Two days later the body of the man who made the future, with few but his close relations following it, went the same way. One to be soon forgotten. The other to be remembered so long as men tell stories.

Saint Bakeoven

I DON'T pretend to be musical, apart, of course, from knowing a good tune when I hear it – the sort of thing that a fellow can whistle in his bath. It does so happen however, that I was almost responsible for what might have been one of the musical sensations of the century, and, before I forget it, I'd better make some record of it for future generations.

I used to spend a part of each year fishing in Kerry in those days. On one occasion, while I was returning from a mountain lake, I ran into a terrific thunderstorm. Below me in the valley I spotted an isolated farmhouse and I worked my way down to it as quickly as possible. I had barely knocked at the door when it was opened by an old man who ushered me in as though I were the prodigal son returning home. He helped me off with my coat, drew up a chair to the fire for me, and, in general, treated me with even more eager hospitality than you usually meet in Kerry.

"You must find it a bit lonely tucked away back here," I suggested, once the preambles of hospitality were settled.

"Yerra – lonely, is it?" replied the old man, whose name, by the way, was Johnny Quill. "The divil a bit lonely am I ever," he went on. "To tell God's truth, 'tis just the other way about."

"How come?" I quite naturally asked, considering the situation of the place.

"'Tis the fairies," he replied, in a matter of fact way. "Them divils do be at me, pestering and worrying and annoying and bothering me all hours of the day and night. 'Tis only when a Christian, such as yourself, comes along, that the sight of him drives them out and I have a bit of peace and ease for myself as it is now. But the moment you'll be gone them divils will be back again with their whispering and their rustling like mice round a corn bin. They have me patience worn out. There should be a law passed against them by those useless people up in Dublin and then put the police onto them. But, oh, no – they're much too busy passing laws to make hens lay eggs by Act of Parliament to have the time to do anything useful. I tell you that the fairies are the plaguiest, most pestering and bewildering form of creation that man was ever burdened with."

"Yes," I agreed, for, after all an old man's fancies break no bones. "I am sure that you must find them a bit of a nuisance."

"Nuisance! Nuisance!" bellowed Johnny. "Why, the divils have me near driven mad. I lambaste them with the handle of a broom. I give them a histe of my boot and a skelp of my tongue, but it's all a waste of energy. A few minutes later and they will be back at their old comether again: whispering hocus pocus; mislaying things and upsetting things on me. There's all classes of them," he continued, "but there is one of them – the plaguiest one of me whole pick of divils, who comes mainly by night. A sort of a foreigner I'd say he would be and a damned bad-tempered one at that. There's some of them all mischief but with this one the game is all music. Whenever he puts his face inside the kitchen the whole house does be filled with the sound of music as though it was the air of the place. Then he tries to be telling me something but I can't make head or tail of the queer language he speaks and that only seems to make him madder and he shakes the great head of him and holds the great fists of him in the air, with the fingers spread out like a dealer trying to buy a beast in a fair for ten pounds from a slow witted man."

" 'Saint! Saint! Saint!' he yells. Then 'Bakeoven! Bakeoven! Bakeoven!' and I can't make sense of that at all for the divil a bit does he look like a saint and the divil a bit do I know what he means by his 'Bakeoven' unless it be one of these newfangled fakes that they have in the towns for the lazy women to bake in."

"To hell with you and your 'bakeoven'," I yell at him, "if it's a 'bakeoven' that you are trying to sell me or persuade me to buy. It was on the cake from the bastable pot that I was reared and on the same I'll finish my days. Then the music starts all over again till my head is like a hive of bees ready to swarm with the sound of it."

"All very interesting," I agreed. "It looks as though the worst of the storm is over. I think that I'll be pushing on." I said goodbye to Johnny and thanked him, and, as far as I was concerned, that would have been the end of the business, for fairies aren't particularly in my line.

It so happened however, that there was a professor of music johnny, from Oxford, staying in the hotel, collecting "folk music", whatever that may be. Naturally he was a difficult subject for conversation and that night I happened to mention the rigmarole Johnny had told me that day, by way of being sociable.

The professor johnny, whose name was Peterson, pricked up his ears almost immediately and showed more signs of life than I had seen so far in him when I told him the yarn. I went away to bed and naturally had forgotten all about it by the following morning but it seemed that this fellow Peterson had, overnight, made a mountain of the story. He had worked out some crazy notion from it about a German composer called Beethoven, who had composed nine symphonies and died before he had finished his tenth; and he had come back in ghost form to worry poor old Johnny Quill about it.

Peterson had worked out that Johnny's "Saint" was the German for "tenth" and his "Bakeoven" was really "Beethoven" – the composer's name, and the music Johnny heard, was, of course, the music of the tenth symphony, now finished. It didn't seem to be dripping with sense to me.

I happened to go into the bar before lunch for an appetiser and who should be there but Johnny Quill himself, celebrating a deal in sheep. We had a drink together and I left him to it and went off in search of food. But in the dining room I ran into Peterson, bubbling over with some new brainwave on Johnny's story. In the hope of finishing the matter off, as far as I was concerned, I led him out and introduced him to Johnny himself, the fount of inspiration. But it wasn't my lucky day, for in spite of his knowledge of music he could not make anything of Johnny's accent, no more than Johnny could make of his, so I had to stand in as interpreter.

I opened the ball with the first round of drinks, Peterson having lemonade and going straight into action, instructing me to ask Johnny to describe the appearance of the ghost or fairy or whatever it was, in detail.

"Tell him," said Johnny, "that he is a stout block of a bucko with a great stook of hair on his head as though he is in dispute with the barber – and that might well be, for he has a fierce, bad tempered jowl on him. His clothes? . . . Yerra, he does mostly wear some sort of an ould swally tail coat with an ould choker round his neck and the knee breeches they used to wear in the time of the caroline hats."

"Hm!" snorted Peterson, like the man who had found the piece of kidney in the pie, when I translated this for him. "Ask him now what language his fairy or whatever it is speaks."

"The divil be from me but how would I know that," replied Johnny. "Tell the man of the lemonade that 'tis neither English nor Irish but some gibberish makeup of his own and that the only words that I can make out at all are his 'Saint' and his 'Bakeoven', and to hell with him and his 'bakeovens'. I'll stick to me bastable pot."

Peterson was studying Johnny intently as he put him through the third degree. "Ask him now," ordered

Peterson, "if anyone else sees this apparition or hears the music."

"Only the divil himself could answer that," snorted Johnny, "but 'tis not likely for ould Bakeoven wouldn't have the time left to be annoying anyone else after all the time that he spends annoying me. He'd scarcely have the time left to wash himself . . . and will you add to that," Johnny continued, "that I will answer no more questions till the gentleman puts away the lemonade and has a glass of whiskey with me like a Christian."

Peterson, in spite of protests, had to yield. Johnny, as the oracle, could call the tune and he called it quickly.

"Would it be possible for me to hear the music and see this ghost if I went along to the house?" was Peterson's next query.

"It might and it might not," was Johnny's answer to this. "But mostly I'd be saying against it for I do notice that when anyone comes into the house to me the music stops and ould Bakeoven goes up the chimney or out of the window. But tell the gentleman that he's welcome anytime and if he can salt the ould divil and take him away with him to foreign parts there will be no man was ever so welcome."

The party spirit was getting into its stride by now. Peterson disappeared for a few minutes and I was hoping that we could adjourn *sine die* but it wasn't to be. He had only been up to his room and he returned with an illustrated history of music. He instructed me to hand it to Johnny and to tell him to look through it and to see if there was a picture in it at all like his "fairy".

Johnny licked his thumb and started to turn the pages one by one. I did not translate all his remarks and comments on the pictures of famous composers he saw, though they were amusing. I had doubts if this Peterson fellow had any sense of humour at all.

After thumbing about half way through the book Johnny let out a yell, putting his finger down on a picture of Beethoven.

"The pesky ould divil himself," he whooped. "The living split image of him! Saint Bakeoven and the great ugly puss of him!" At this Peterson went up in the air. He ordered another round of drinks immediately. Even I began to wonder if there might be something in it after all.

"Ask him now," said Peterson, as pleased as Punch, "if he could describe or remember the music he hears."

"Could I remember the music!" exclaimed Johnny. "Indeed, but it would be the day of the greatest aise to me when the day dawns that I disremember every screech of it. As for describing of it," he continued, after some head-scratching, "will you tell him that it would be beyond the powers of the worst poet yet born to put words to it. 'Tis such a roaring and a buzzing and a banging and a beating: such a twirling of trumpets and a tweaking of flutes and a scattering of the scraping of fiddles that the like of it was never heard before in the history of the world. 'Tis like the bellowings of dumb animals in pain and the howling of infants in divilment and the scolding of women in crossness and in the midst of it all there is this ould divil of a queer one, waving his hands up and down and about in the air as though the sound was all running out of the ends of his fingers, like porter out of a tap."

"Only once did I hear the match of it in my life and that was in the days of the ould militia in the town of Kenmare when someone had treated the band with decency and the band had treated themselves with equal decency and they marched through the town 'stocious' and every man of them doing his best to outblow the other fellow."

Johnny now ordered a round and Peterson replied with another question, asking if Johnny could hum or whistle the music or give some actual idea of it. Johnny was now most ready to oblige.

"I'd give you more than an idea of it, with a heart and a half, and good riddance to it," said he, "but that it is a class of music that has no sense at all to it at all at all. 'Tis what you might call a porridge of a music – not like the 'Blackbird' or 'The Coolin' or 'The Wind that Shakes the Barley' or any of the decent civilised tunes that wake a man's heart and set his feet tapping. But I will do the best I can to accommodate the gentleman for he is turning out to be a better class of a man than my first judgment of him. 'Tis something like this that it goes."

With that Johnny drained his glass, threw back his head, fixed his eye on a spot on the ceiling and started to screech and to bawl and to roar and to groan until, after a couple of minutes, even Peterson, with all his interest in music, had had enough of Johnny Quill's version of Beethoven's Tenth Symphony. It was a thirst-provoking effort and Peterson thought the game worth while but demanded a *quid* for his *quo*.

"Ask him if there is any musical instrument that he can play with which he might be able to reproduce some of the music he hears."

After probing into the nature of Johnny's polite accomplishments, the only thing that I could discover was that when he was young – and that was a long time ago – he had been able to play the bagpipes – but not very well. About here the party broke up.

The following morning, when Peterson had recovered after a good night's sleep, he had worked out a plan of campaign, for there wasn't any doubt now in his mind, on the circumstantial evidence so far produced. He was on the verge of the most amazing musical discovery of the century. The weather wasn't too good for fishing and as there wasn't much else to do I continued as *aide de camp* and general adviser and interpreter.

The first thing that we did was to visit Johnny's house and we soon found that we were quite definitely not allergic to fairies. Even Peterson did not hear a note.

According to Johnny the moment we entered the house both the fairy and his music faded away. Naturally Peterson was a bit hurt about this but he was quite certain that Johnny was speaking the truth and quite incapable of pulling Peterson's leg on his home ground, as you might say.

This meant that we had to fall back on Johnny himself as medium, interpreter or what you will. And that meant that, by hook or crook, he would have to reproduce what he heard by means of the only musical instrument he knew – the bagpipes. Peterson wasn't at all in favour of my suggestion, my quite practical suggestion, of bringing a band along and letting Johnny conduct it. He even suspected that I was pulling his leg and not treating the matter with sufficient gravity.

So the problem, or rather the practical solution to it, was narrowed down to bagpipes. Somewhere in the district there was reputed to be a pair or set or whatever it is of them but when it came to finding them they were as elusive as the end of a rainbow, flitting ahead of us from valley to valley and house to house. At last we caught up with them. Johnny regarded them carefully, seriously and ruefully. With all his native gift of courtesy he could find little good to say about them. There was a whistle or a tweeter or some such vital part missing. One of the protruding flutes or whatever they were was most obviously cracked. More apparent still was a great rent in the windbag. But, with optimism, a dash of glue, some twine and wire, a splash of tar and a bit of an old tyre, Johnny thought that he might be able to make a job of them.

Eventually, with the help of the 'smith and the carpenter and a man who was a great hand at tying a fly and another man who had an uncle in America who, in his day had been a famous piper, so that he had claims to being an expert, one place removed, we got the contraption fixed up. As Johnny tactfully described it –

53

"they worked in a kind of a class of a way." Now all that he needed was a few days' practice to get his wind and fingers into trim.

The appointed night arrived and with it rain in sheets and floods and torrents. This seemed to me to be a warning to let well alone and sleeping spirits lie. It seemed just any other kind of night rather than one to set off into the darkness and the wetness of a desolate mountain valley to hear the first performance of a symphony played on bagpipes – or played any way at all for that matter. Peterson's mind however was made up and I decided that being in for a penny I might as well be in for a pound.

We borrowed the hotel proprietor's car. I took along a bottle of whiskey and a couple of rugs. As luggage Peterson had a wad of music paper. Long before we arrived at the concert hall it was obvious, even above the storm, that Johnny had entered into the spirit of the occasion and was already having a preliminary canter. It seems that somehow the fairy or ghost had got an inkling of what was in the wind and had readily co-operated with the notion. In fact they had already a dress rehearsal and come to a common understanding of the procedure to be adopted. Beethoven would conduct a few bars and while they still lingered in Johnny's ears he would have a skirl or whatever the musical term is for a dash at it and so they would progress from bar to bar.

Johnny himself was by this time so taken up with the idea and the possible hope of ridding himself of his musical lodger, that he was taking the matter almost as seriously as Peterson himself. He wouldn't even have a drink before we started. "Only a dart, now and again, of the purest of spring water," he said, pointing to a bottle at his side, "just for the wind's sake, until the gentleman is satisfied."

Still we were not *personae gratae* with fairies and while we were within the kitchen Johnny said there would not be a note of music. When you think of all the trouble that Peterson was giving himself and other people it did really seem a bit inconsiderate on the part of Beethoven, but judging by the picture of him it was about what you might be led to expect from him. So it meant that we – or rather Peterson – would have to eavesdrop through the window.

I, never having been much of an enthusiast for symphonies or bagpipes, retired to the shelter of the car. I wrapped myself up in the rugs and opened the bottle of whiskey. Unfortunately I was still within earshot of the bedlam which was let loose when the performance started, but as the storm increased the howling of the wind and the lashing rain toned it down somewhat. There would be a squealing and a screeching from the kitchen as though a score of pigs were being slaughtered. There was Peterson huddled up against the window ledge, with the rain cascading over him from the roof, while he scribbled down crotchets and quavers. Now and again he would bawl through the window for a repeat. Now and again there would be a lull in the noise, as Johnny took a swig of the purest spring water for his wind's sake.

Mercifully after a short while I fell into a dose. What woke me wasn't a noise. It was the absence of a noise. I came to, conscious that now there was only the howling of the wind and the roar of the swollen mountain torrents around me. There wasn't a sound from Johnny's kitchen. The door was open and Peterson was missing. I made a dash for the house to find Johnny on the flat of his back on the floor, as he would describe it, "stocious". The bottle of the "finest of spring water" lay smashed beside him and from the trickle which was left in it there came a smell which might be mistaken for whiskey. It is not unknown in Kerry where so many improbable things seem to be possible for "the finest of spring water" to have such a smell. Beside the fragments of the bottle lay the corpse of the bagpipes in a heap.

"Busht! Busht and be damned!" were Johnny's last words as he gave himself up to the soundest sleep that ever fell on any man. The description aptly covered all – Johnny, the bottle and the bagpipes. We made Johnny comfortable for the night in his bed. There was nothing more that we could do. The performance was ended. The carriage awaited at the door.

Peterson was quite happy but very wet. There wasn't a doubt now in his mind. It was the true, authentic Beethoven music alright, recognisable even through the medium of bagpipes. A few score nights such as this and he would have the whole thing down in crotchets and .quavers. A few months of work on it and it would be ready to astonish the world.

It seemed unfortunate that Peterson developed a high temperature during the night and had to be rushed off to a nursing home the following morning with pneumonia. But all's well that ends well and a few days later Johnny himself had to be taken to the county hospital. The combination of the finest of spring water, the excitement and the strenuous exercises of bagpipe blowing had not been the best treatment for the heart at his age. So, as it turned out, Peterson would not have been able to do anything more, and anyway the bagpipes were quite beyond any further repair.

I had quite a busy time between the two invalids: writing letters for Peterson, when he turned the corner, and doing a few odd things for Johnny. The doctor had advised Johnny to stay on in the hospital and he wasn't at all unwilling. I arranged the settling of his bit of land to a relative so that Johnny would be able to draw the old age pension and so have no further worry.

As soon as Peterson was well enough I drove him over to see Johnny and, needless to say, Peterson had only one interest in the visit.

"Ould Bakeoven and his music? . . . Yerra, thank God that I have neither sight nor sound of him since the blessed day that I came in here – and good riddance, for at last after all these years I have peace and ease for myself and

56

am able to call my soul my own."

"But, manalive!" almost shrieked Peterson, "don't you remember the music?"

"The divil a note of it," answered Johnny, puffing contentedly away at his pipe. "The divil a note of it have I heard since I came in and the divil a note of it will I hear to the end of my days for I have handed the place and the cow and the sheep to a nephew of mine and I have no mind to budge from here till they carry me out feet foremost. I'll live the rest of my life like a fine civil servant, at the country's expense, taking my aise like a lord, instead of being at the beck and call of a pack of fairies like a boots in an hotel."

Peterson cajoled, bribed, bullied, pleaded, wheedled and argued but Johnny would listen to no argument and no persuasion. The last thing that he said to Peterson when we came to say goodbye was: "If you should happen to see Ould Bakeoven at any time during your travels will you tell him from me that I did him a great harm and a great injustice and that I am sorry for it, for after all he was right. 'Tis the new-fangled 'bakeovens' that they use in this place for their breadmaking and you never in all your life tasted sweeter or grander or nuttier bread."

Circe

WERE you in Grafton Street on the morning of the last Friday of September in 1973? I think it was the 27th. . . . If you were, though I know that it is a long time ago, you may remember it by the fact that you experienced a curious and quite unexpected sensation which will have marked it in your mind. The experience was that of a sudden intense gust of a scent or odour, coming right out of the blue. It may have been the scent of violets, of cooking meat, of ginger, or any of a score or more distinctive odours, powerful enough, unexpected enough, to pull your attention up short.

Whether you in particular can remember this or not, there were many hundreds of people in the vicinity of Grafton Street on that morning who did have such an experience. And it was an actual experience and not a freak of the senses or a trick of the individual mind. It was the result of a planned experiment. An experiment which, in relation to the present state of mankind, was perhaps too previous.

A few months before this incident in Grafton Street I met a man whom I shall call Circe. That, obviously, was not his real name, but, as I think that you will come to learn, an appropriate pseudonymn. The meeting between us had been arranged by a common acquaintance, knowing that Circe and I shared an interest – an interest in the sense of smell.

Circe, who was a wealthy man, had a large estate about thirty miles from the city. He claimed to have developed an electronic means for the production of odours. I myself was engaged on a thesis relating to the evocative power of scent on deeply buried memories. Naturally enough the possibility of working with artificially produced odour interested me greatly – if it was true.

If it was true. That, according to the knowledge of the time, seemed highly improbable and, to me, Circe had the looks and the manner of a charlatan. He was gross, flabby, arrogant and self-satisfied. I took an immediate dislike – a prejudiced dislike – towards him. He wanted some temporary assistance from someone with an interest in the subject of his claim. Though sceptical and prejudiced, I swallowed both and agreed to go down for at least a demonstration of his claims and, if I was satisfied, to work with him.

Sceptical as I was, on my first introduction to what Circe called his "box of tricks" my scepticism was shattered. The "box of tricks" was a small cabinet on the front of which was a series of dials, meters and switches. It would have passed for some modern medical appliance, or chemical apparatus, or even a radio set.

Circe, after introducing me to the apparatus, immediately demonstrated it to me with a showman's aplomb. "Actions speak louder than words. An ounce of practice is worth a pound of preaching." He inserted a key and switched the contraption on. He adjusted one of the dials on the front panel. Instantly the room was filled with the scent of new mown grass. After a moment he turned the dial back and the perfume vanished. There wasn't a trace of it. It was, by analogy, as though at one moment the room had been brilliantly lit and then, at the turn of a switch, been plunged into total darkness. I didn't believe it, of course.

He repeated the demonstration after making some other dial movements. Once again, in an instant, the room was filled with perfume, this time that of violets. Again, after a minute's interval, he snapped the switch and the perfume had vanished utterly. Then after some further adjustment he activated the instrument once more. Now the atmosphere was laden with the scent of apple-blossom. His hand was on one of the dials. He moved it slowly. The intensity of the scent grew. He moved it further. The scent became almost solid and substantial. It was now so intense that it had become overpowering and nauseating so that I was on the point of physical sickness. Then, with his eyes on me, he flicked the instrument off. I did not know what had happened to me. Body and mind were out of step. The apple-blossom scent was no longer there. There was no trace of it. That a moment ago the room had been filled with it to the point of nausea was a trick of the imagination.

My scepticism put up a vain fight. The demonstration was incredible – but smelling is believing. By some conjuring trick Circe might have flooded the room with the various scents. That was difficult to imagine, but nevertheless it was possible. But, allowing that, what was not possible was that in an instant the atmosphere of the room could have been totally rid of the perfume. Not once alone but several times. Even just the once was impossible. We have no experience of instantaneous odours. A basic element of them is their lingering or persistent quality.

If this was all true and not a remarkable bit of conjuring, Circe was on to something revolutionary and fundamental. It amounted to a tremendous breakthrough in the scrappy and tentative science of osmics or the sense of smell.

The science was vague and tentative for the simple reason that there was no known means of actually creating or generating a scent from a controlled energy transformation, as we can do, for instance, with light and sound. The only materials on which the science could work were naturally occurring odiferous substances. Why and how they were odiferous was entirely hypothetical. One hypothesis was that such substances were composed of molecules of characteristic shape. These molecules, when diluted and carried in the atmosphere, fitted, as keys into a lock, in similarly shaped holes in the olfactory organ and by so doing each produced its own particular sensation of odour.

Circe's instrument, if it was genuine, completely controverted this hypothesis and seemed closer to another, again quite tentative, that a particular odour sensation was brought about by characteristic molecular vibrations sensed by a mechanism in the sense organ.

The demonstration impressed and fascinated me. Circe discussed it with pride and interest. He admitted readily that it was not, basically, his own invention and all that he had done with it so far amounted to little more than practical and mechanical improvements on it. The story he told me of its origin was almost as extraordinary as the demonstration itself.

Some years ago he had been working in the University of Prague. There he had become friendly with an electronics engineer who was working on ultra high frequency radiation. In the ultra high frequency band he had come across a very narrow area which was affected by, he thought at first, dust in the air, and then he found that it was any form of scent or odour. Pursuing this he discovered that the radiation in this extremely narrow band itself affected the organ of smell. On this ground he had devised an apparatus which itself generated odour and which he had refined so that he was able to radiate differentiated odours at will. This was the apparatus which Circe had demonstrated to me.

The next chapter of the story has the elements of the stock thriller. Circe and the engineer shared a flat. One night Russian agents broke into the flat and kidnapped the engineer and also the instrument. Neither man nor machine have been heard of since. Circe knew that there was a duplicate of the apparatus in the university. Acting quickly he got hold of it, and now, its importance having been dramatically emphasised, he decided to get it out of the country before the Russians could get it and so save the important knowledge for the West.

Surmounting all the fantastic difficulties which are the essential ingredients of such a story, Circe succeeded at last in getting both himself and the machine to the safety and security of Ireland. I only half swallowed this and, in any case, to me all this seemed to be of minor importance. I agreed to work with Circe and give what help I could. Circe himself had quite a solid knowledge of electronics. My role lay more in my knowledge of perfumes, smells and their chemistry and categories.

So, for several weeks we worked. Amongst other things we did was to devise a method of beaming the radiations. The experiment we made in Grafton Street was one outcome of this. We took the apparatus up to Dublin in an open lorry and, from the corners of side streets, beamed scents and odours, like a searchlight, at the passers by, with a cine camera synchronised with the beaming to record their facial reactions. We also did controlled and measured experiments in intensity and compiled a tabulation of dial readings in relation to specific odours. From this we were able to work out mixes, as it were, to create any desired scent or smell from the synthesis of the basic odours.

Whatever we did was done together. I was never allowed to handle the instrument on my own. It was energised by a lock and key and Circe always kept the key in his pocket. I couldn't really complain. After all, the whole thing was his. Still, it did strike me as a bit odd.

Naturally during the course of working together we discussed almost every aspect of what amounted to the new science which we were creating. The word "almost" is important. One day I questioned Circe about investigating the fringes of the electronic spectrum on which the work was based.

"There are no fringes," Circe replied brusquely.

"But there must be fringes beyond the threshold of human conscious perception – those wavelengths perceptible to animals and insects – the dog, for instance."

"There are no fringes. There may be in nature but not in this artificial simulation."

"But surely there is a parallel with light and sound? There can't be a sudden and absolute cut-off?"

"I have told you that there are no fringes and there is no one who can know that better than I."

The way this was said indicated that the topic was definitely not discussable. For some reason the subject of the fringes of the phenomenon were *verboten* and I had been warned. It was very stupid of him. It was stupid in more ways than one. It was stupid of him to believe that I would accept such an absurd dictat without a reasonable explanation. It was stupid of him not to see that by such an answer he was drawing attention to something, whatever it might be, which he wanted to conceal – the matter of the fringes, obviously. It was the stupidity which was the product of that arrogance that I had immediately noticed about him – or vice versa.

I stifled my suspicion. I made no further reference to the *verboten* subject but I did quite a lot of thinking both about the fringes and about Circe.

I had a room in Circe's large house which was run by a housekeeper and I had most of my meals with him so that I learnt quite a lot about him as a man. My impression of his arrogance was confirmed almost daily. He was a great admirer of both Hitler and Stalin and frequently quoted Nietchze. That told me an amount. I quickly gathered that, on the whole, he didn't like the human race but rather despised it, particularly for its obese stupidity. That amused me quietly. Then it seemed strange that he did not want or seek and practically forbade any public or scientific interest in the remarkable invention which was in his possession.

Sometimes in the evenings I went for a walk and called in to the pub in the village for a drink. After my first visit when I mentioned that I was doing some work for Circe I found that on my next visit I was more or less cold shouldered, despite the usual welcome accorded to a stranger. By chance the publican himself happened to be from my own county and one night when he was alone I asked him what I had done to be more or less ostracised.

With a degree of reluctance he explained that it was most probably because the men in the bar knew that I was working with or a friend or acquaintance of Circe's, and Circe had not too good a name locally. For the moment no reason was given. That in itself puzzled me, for obviously Circe employed quite a number of men about the place as handymen, gardeners and so on.

It took a week or two to get any further detail. Then I was told that Circe was bad news in the district. Two men at least had suffered in health as the result of working for him and had not yet got the better of it. In some way their minds had been affected and they had to be admitted to the county mental hospital. Of course it could have been a coincidence, but that was not accepted. There was something about Circe. As the result of local opinion no one in the locality now worked for him and he had to staff the place with anyone he could – even men he picked up wandering the roads.

Prejudice, suspicion, resentment wrestled with interest. Several times I was on the point of leaving altogether but always interest won the day. Now added to interest – in the immediate sense of the novelty of the work in which I participated – was the added interest, or curiosity, about the origin of Circe's local bad name, or "bad news" as it was put.

The more that I brooded over the muddy situation the more I felt certain that it had something to do with the matter of the *verboten* "fringes". The more I considered "fringes" and let my imagination – and my reason – loose on this aspect, the more I came to realise how important, now that odour could be artificially produced, these fringes might be and how an investigation of them might offer explanations to many hidden aspects of life.

That there are such fringes to the domain of the sense of smell is without question. It may be that in pre-civilised man the sense of smell played a much greater part in his life and had a much wider compass, but civilisation has repressed much of the sense and left us with only a very narrow range which even now is rapidly dwindling. Nature and evolution had some purpose in this suppression and perhaps on the whole it was for our good and progress. But are these fringes still operative in our unconscious? Are they still effective and a power in our lives unknown to us? May not many of our moods, our despairs and exultations, be the result of them? Do they still affect our judgments and our prejudices, unknown to us?

I wanted to know and the only way to find out was to make an experiment with the apparatus and I would have to do that without Circe knowing. The key to that was the key which he always kept in his pocket. I had to get hold of it in some way, and my conscience was getting more tolerant about the means as each day passed. With hope, I got some impression wax and kept it in a small tin in my pocket. An opportunity might arise when Circe was absent from the laboratory for sufficient time to allow me to whip out the key and press it into the wax and get an impression of it from which I could get a duplicate copy. The switch was an ordinary car ignition switch. But the opportunity was the difficulty. There was an extension phone in the laboratory. Casual callers were rare. Circe, though stupid, was wary enough and I dared not rouse his suspicion.

Then nature intervened. During a morning session Circe suddenly let out a roar, jumped out of his chair and beat at his leg. Then another yell and he dashed into the bathroom. There was time enough to whip the key out of the switch, press it into the wax and return it before I hastened, with a bewildered anxiety, to Circe's assistance. A torpid wasp had crept up his leg and stung him on the back of his knee. That afternoon I went to a garage and had no difficulty in getting a key which settled snugly into the wax matrix.

Another week passed before Circe was called to Dublin concerning one of his many business interests. He announced that he would be staying overnight. He of course took the instrument key and locked the door – I suppose against the KGB. I had examined the old-fashioned window latch and saw that it could be easily opened and closed with a knife blade. Circe couldn't be expected to think of everything.

I put the key into the switch and energised the instrument. The dial was set so that the radiation lay in the middle range of the familiar odours with which we usually operated. Slowly I turned it up. Slowly the odours became thinner, higher in pitch, more delicate, until there was no longer any consciously perceptible smell. But the instrument was still radiating nevertheless in the fringe beyond normal perception. Though I no longer had any conscious awareness of any odour, my brain and my mind were being affected.

I had, over the years, experimented with the various hallucinogens such as mescal, hashish, Lysergic acid and such. Now my mind was being affected in a similar way to that brought about by these drugs but in a much more distinct and defined way. I moved the dial slowly on. I attained happiness and intense well being. Then, as I shifted the dial, I was transported into rapture and what I can only call ecstasy. As an individual I no longer existed. I was no longer differentiated from my surroundings. It was as though I no longer knew or had thoughts but simply was and had being alone. With an effort I stopped and slowly turned the dial back again and retraced the way which I had come – through the airy fragrances associated with spring to the fuller scents of the summer and then to the heavy rich, musky smells which we associate with the East.

Now the room was being filled with foetid, nauseating

stenches which passed into the smells of decay, putrifaction and corruption, until all sensation of smell faded out of consciousness. I slowly and fearfully moved the dial further and the radiation was still effective, but now directly affecting my brain and my mind with hideous nightmares and feelings of bestiality which it would be wrong to associate with the beasts. Describable sensation and thought vanished, and I can only describe the next stage as that of being completely – almost completely – possessed by evil. It was not any sense of wrongdoing but of a power which was beyond both evil and good and was meaningless on that level. I was afraid. I was fascinated. I was terrified. I knew that I had reached the limit of even my momentary subjection. Though I had not yet reached the limit of the scale I turned back through all the natural disgusts, distastes and revulsions of everyday life to the point on the dial where I had started.

In both experiments I had made use of the apparatus and its radiations at almost its lowest intensity or power. I could have amplified this whole range of experience one hundredfold at least. I had only touched on the surface of its potentialities and a fraction of its power, yet at both ends I had experienced that which I can never forget – at one end the approach to hell and at the other the approach to heaven. I have to live in this world which lies between.

I had had enough. I had found out about the fringes and that there *were* fringes and what the effect of these fringes was and what they could be. I switched the instrument off and withdrew the key. I left the room as I had found it and got out again through the window into fresh air. I went for a long walk.

Some, not all, of the bits and pieces fitted together. I saw a reason why Circe so stupidly denied the existence of the fringes. At least it was reasonable if there was justification for the name which he had earned in the village and that he was responsible for two men going mad and another killing himself. Then that linked itself with his arrogance, his worship of power and for his idols such as Hitler, Stalin and Nietzsche. He had, by a freak of chance, got hold of an instrument or tool which, rightly used, could enlarge mankind's knowledge of itself enormously. He had, I was forced to believe, seen it merely as a means to the enhancement of his own personal power over men.

But supposing that this was true, what could I do about it? I did not feel sufficiently self-righteous to destroy the box of tricks. It was even possible that if I did Circe had sufficent knowledge to reconstruct it. I could not involve the co-operation of anyone else for, without actual experience, who would believe me? If I challenged Circe in any way he would just laugh at me and carry on.

At the end of the week I had to go to my sister's wedding and I was away for four days. I returned reluctantly and with a feeling of incompetence and weakness. The four days absence had offered me no solution and had merely increased my feeling of impotence. I knew so much and could do so little.

It was well after midnight by the time that I got back. Passing up the drive I saw a light in the laboratory, though this was not unusual, for Circe often worked on his own at night. But as I reached the house I saw that the curtains were not drawn and, moreover, there was a great jagged hole in the window itself. For a moment I thought of Russians. I got out of the car and walked over the lawn to investigate.

Through the broken window I saw that the whole interior of the laboratory had been wrecked. Crouched in a corner was Circe, covered in blood, his eyes blazing and bloodshot. Then he let out a roar and hurled himself, blindly and savagely, at a cabinet, battering at it with his torn and gashed hands from which the blood was pouring, until he had smashed it to pieces.

I ran into the house and phoned the hospital for the ambulance and told them to bring at least two strong attendants and a strait jacket for a violent case. When it arrived we broke down the locked door and rushed in. Circe confronted us, looking like a gorilla which had gone berserk. In spite of a broken arm and several other injuries, four of us had an enormous job to overpower him and lash him down to a stretcher.

Everything in the place was smashed. Blood was spattered everywhere. The apparatus lay on the floor, irretrievably broken, trampled on, destroyed. In the chaos I could find no clue as to what might have happened. Circe had been alone. The door was locked. No one could have got into the room through the jagged hole in the window pane. I had an idea of what had happened but I could not imagine how it had happened.

Three days later Circe died. Though the doctors in the hospital had done all that they possibly could for him, he had already done himself irreparable damage. The only way in which they could account for his state was that he had suffered a most violent brainstorm.

I stayed on for a few days and did what I could to help the housekeeper to get in touch with Circe's relations and clear up his affairs. I went down to the pub for a final drink. Of course what had happened was the whole topic of conversation and there wasn't more than a very nominal sympathy for Circe. In fact it was regarded as a case of what is called "poetic justice". Circe had got what was coming to him. He had been paid in his own coin.

There was one small matter which, for a moment, created some discussion. It was not until the day after Circe was taken away that someone noticed that one of the handymen employed about the place, by the name of Tom, had vanished. There was vague speculation, in the attempt to solve the mystery, as to the possibility that Tom's sudden disappearance may have had some bearing on the matter. But I was in the position to nullify that. The door was locked. Circe himself, in his frenzy, had broken the window and anyway how could Tom have caused Circe's brainstorm? My explanation ended any further speculation in that direction.

I left and took up my normal life once again. Away from the actual scene, away from the immediate engagement of the past few months, I gained a perspective view of the whole matter. My experience and what I had learnt became much more significant than the detail of Circe's death.

If Circe was to be believed the Russians had a duplicate of the destroyed instrument and it would be reasonable to assume that they had, in the meantime, worked on it and developed it further. But discounting Circe's thriller, the fact remained that the olfactory sense could be stimulated electronically. Much more important was the fact, which I had experienced in small degree, that the non-conscious thresholds of this sense which this artificial stimulus could affect had a profound effect on the human mind and through that on the human personality. This artificial means opened up an entirely new way of investigation and research into the evolution, the composition and functioning of the human mind.

I knew, but I had not one shred of evidence to prove what I knew. Though I was in touch with the very few biochemists, physiologists and psychologists interested in the sense of smell, they were all content enough to make do with the present vague hypothesis relating to it. In any case, the domain was of such little importance that it could be considered almost wholly academic. In current terms perhaps it was valued lowly in interest because there was no obvious money in it. Though I knew its possible importance I was quite powerless to convince anyone else, least of all anyone with sufficient interest and authority to pay serious heed to me.

I even spent some time studying electronics in the hope that I might be able to rig up some crude form of demonstration to prove what I knew. I got nowhere and I could get no practical help in the particular and limited direction in which I was interested without declaring my eventual aim. If I did that, I knew that the help would dry up. There would be a shrug of the shoulders and I would become someone else with a bee in his bonnet.

Two years passed and to rid myself of the sense of frustration I undertook more than enough work to leave me little time for brooding and adding to my sense of helplessness. One day I stopped at an hotel in the South for lunch. I went into the bar for a drink beforehand. There was one man sitting alone there.

I ordered my drink and glanced at him. There was something very vaguely familiar about him but I could not immediately place him. He finished his drink and started to walk away from the bar with a slight, rather curious, limp which triggered my memory. I called to him "Tom?" He swung round and looked at me, hesitantly for a moment, before he replied. "Doctor Lawton?"

I asked him to have a drink and then, over lunch, told him, in general, what had happened about Circe without any reference to his own disappearance. I gave him the official version of Circe's death as the result of an intense brainstorm.

"I suppose there was some wondering about my sudden out?"

"Yes, of course there was, but that obviously could have had nothing to do with it. I believe that you had been talking all that week of clearing off."

"Yes, I did intend to chuck it up. My brother was home from Canada on holiday. He had been out there for three years, working on oil rigs, and he had been at me to go back with him. There was sure work. Pretty tough conditions but wonderful pay." There was a silence before he continued. "You say that Circe went mad as the result of something that happened to his brain?" Again a silence.

"I'd better tell you and get it off my mind. . . . I did have something to do with it. It was because of that that I skipped suddenly . . . but I didn't kill Circe."

He told me another aspect of the happening. Circe had

asked him one evening to do some small carpentry job on a filing cabinet in the laboratory. He showed him what he wanted and then left him but he kept coming in and out and fiddling with that radio set or whatever it was he had. The job didn't amount to much and anyway he didn't seem to be over-interested in it. Tom got suspicious about the in and out business and the fiddling with the silent radio. He'd heard some of the talk amongst the locals about Circe which increased his suspicion. Circe began to get annoyed. Still he tried to keep Tom in the laboratory with one excuse after another and all the time twiddling away at the set and running in and out like a scattered hen.

Tom had had enough of it. It was obvious enough to him now that the repair job was only a blind to keep him there for some reason. He closed his fist and let Circe have it on the point of the jaw and skipped pulling the door closed after him. He knew there would be hell to pay in the morning so he took his leave prematurely that night.

There was something missing in his story.

"You didn't feel any effect — any sort of queer feeling while you were working?"

"No. Nothing except every moment I was getting more and more suspicious of what Circe had me there for, for it wasn't the job on the cabinet. That was only an excuse."

"You didn't feel sick or anything?"

"I felt nothing except myself getting madder and madder till I socked him."

There was a vase of azaleas on the lunch table. I drew them towards me and buried my nose in them. Then I pushed the vase over towards Tom.

"I think those have the most delicate perfume of all the early flowers."

Tom pushed the vase back to me with a smile.

"Means nothing to me. I was born without a sense of smell."

That was what was missing. Circe had, by chance, picked a wrong guinea pig. He could have turned the set

72

on to its full intensity but Tom would not have been affected any more than a blind man would have been affected by a searchlight.

Tom had knocked Circe out and he lay there unconscious but all the time subject himself to the radiation to which he had vainly been subjecting Tom. By the time he became conscious again it had done its ironic work. It had changed Circe into the indescribable creature I had found. He had destroyed the laboratory, the instrument and himself. The odds against an individual being completely anosmic, or without a sense of smell, are large. Circe, arrogant or stupid or over-confident in himself, had backed a wild outsider.

One mystery was solved. Another remains. Was Circe's thriller fact or fiction? Have the Russians a duplicate of the apparatus which killed Circe or was this just a story? Only time will tell.

Book Review

THE re-issue of Professor Bolton's "Europa and the Bull" is welcome and long overdue. It is a work of scholarship which casts an entirely original light on the whole course of Western civilisation by searchlighting the part played in its mythology, religion, literature and history by the bull. The field covered by the work is vast, ranging from the caves of Lascaux through the early kingdoms of the Eastern Mediterranean – Assyria, Egypt and Crete – to modern Spain.

It is unfortunate, however – and difficult to understand why – that Professor Bolton's final chapter and conclusion, which was omitted from the original edition, is still omitted from this re-issue. This chapter he discussed at length with me. He looked upon it as the culmination and consolidation of his life's work. It was sent to the publishers and I have, after the first edition, reminded them of the matter. The continued omission by them is at least cavilier if not contemptuous.

Unfortunately I have no actual copy of the chapter and have only references to it in my letters from Professor Bolton, but I was close enough to him, and in fact a participant in the actual illuminating incident which sparked this final chapter. I feel now that it is my duty to at least record the incident, though I have insufficient scholarship to evaluate it in Bolton's terms and framework. That I must leave to someone more learned.

Professor Bolton was my tutor at St. Marks and we established a friendship which lasted till his death. For, apart from history, we shared a common interest in dry fly fishing. After I inherited Glasheen, in West Cork, he invariably came over during the long vacation to spend a couple of weeks on the excellent Glasheen River. Sport, however, was not his sole interest in Ireland for he took a lively interest in Irish mythology, folklore and history – the "Tain" saga naturally being of prime interest to him.

There was, however, another historical event in modern Irish history which occupied much of his interest during his annual visits. It was the battle of Kinsale. This he regarded as a turning point in modern European history, but he was never completely happy with the accepted versions of the Spanish defeat. He always felt that there was a hidden aspect of it, ignored or neglected or forgotten, which would explain the Spanish defeat more fully than the historical record showed.

His last visit to me happened to be during that year in which the Irish government of the time was making strenuous efforts to establish a sound cattle stock in the country. It was a long overdue reform, for cattle breeding, apart from that of a few of the conscientious and far sighted large farmers, was completely haphazard. Any farmer could keep a bull for breeding without licence or adequate examination and far too many of them did. The motive in the majority of cases was more one of pride rather than profit. The keeping of a bull gave the small farmer a form of prestige. It also produced an abnormally large number of undersized, diseased and uneconomic progeny.

Government intervention in the matter was, naturally, resented, not simply because it was government intervention but also because it was interference with an age-long and God given right and a hurt to proper pride. There were protest meetings at every cross roads. Government inspectors and officials were threatened and harried. There were angry plans for boycott. Ingenious arguments were woven in the pubs from both ancient history and present personalities. Subtle plots were hinted at. There were suggestions of bribery in high places. The notion that there was a different law for the poor than for

75

the rich was mooted. The cry of injustice echoed through the land.

I had imagined that the tense situation which had developed in this matter would interest Professor Bolton when he came on his annual visit. However, it seemed that I was wrong. All the pother concerned actual bulls: bulls in the flesh, not symbolic bulls. I began to credit the quip circulated about him years ago, that, preoccupied with mythological bulls he would not recognise an actual bull if he met one.

Though disinterested in the immediate concern of the neighbourhood, he still maintained his interest in the matter of the battle of Kinsale. In fact the past year's browsing over the matter had only emphasised his suspicion of the veracity of the accepted accounts of the battle. More than ever he felt certain that there was a piece missing − either by oversight or by manipulation − which distorted the historical balance. It may have been some detail trivial at the moment, the significance of which had not been appreciated at the time and the particular detail had been lost in the passage of time. A plan had been devised. It had failed in execution but the reasons given for the failure did not hang together − at least that was Professor Bolton's contention and the source of his dissatisfaction and interest.

On a day too bright for the river we made the short journey to Kinsale as we had done several times in previous years. Bolton had equipped himself with a large scale ordnance map of the locality, copies of a contemporary plan of the seige and battle and field glasses. I halted the car on a byroad overlooking the landing place of the Spanish auxiliary force. Bolton opened out the map on the top of the stone wall and examined the lay of the land beneath us through his field glasses.

You can't do things so unusual as that in the Irish countryside without immediately attracting attention. You are certain to be observed and noticed as strangers alone even though you will be quite unconscious of the fact. The map and the field glasses would stimulate even greater interest.

So, it wasn't long before we observed that we were being observed with particular interest from the small farm below us on the edge of the sea.

Professor Bolton decided that a more intimate examination of the terrain would be helpful. He rolled up the map and tucked it under his arm. We opened a gate and down a boreen to the farm below. As we approached it a burly and angry man, armed with a pitchfork, came round the gable of the house and challenged us.

"Get to hell out of here or I'll puncture the two of ye! Get back to your damned dipartment in Dublin and leave me in peace."

We were, of course – I think the correct word would be – nonplussed. I hastily explained that we had nothing at all to do with Dublin or any department but my explanation was only met with a contemptuous incredulity.

"I can smell ye. If you are not from the dipartment you're dipartment spies. You are plain clothes peelers – spies in disguise." Professor Bolton had that disarming, innocent air common enough amongst scholars.

"I assure you, my good man, that we have nothing whatsoever to do with either departments or the police. We simply came to ask you to allow us to inspect the place on the shore where the Spaniards are reputed to have landed at the battle of Kinsale."

The innocence, the English accent and mention of the Battle of Kinsale gained the day and the farmer's favour for us.

"You have the look and the talk of a decent honest man and I am sorry for the bad manners and the cross talk. And if it's about the Spaniards that you've come you couldn't have come to a more knowledgeable man in the matter for I am John Sullivan – Sullivan of the Bulls. Born so and, with the help of God, will die so. Come now.

Follow me and I will show you the how and the where and the whyfor of the Spaniards and Kinsale. No man better."

So, we followed him across the haggard and down a boreen.

"'Tis a queer ungrateful thing for any government — least of all your own —to be doing to a man, to be robbing him of his name and his fame and with it the name and the fame of all those who went before him. And to make matters worse, when they know, as all men know, that if it wasn't for the Sullivans of the Bull they wouldn't be where they are today and, likely as not, we would all be on a diet of frogs, what's more,"

We came to a gate. Sullivan halted and pointed over the gate to a young bull standing in the middle of the field.

"Isn't he now the beauty of beauties? And he has a couple of years of growing to do yet before he will be in his prime."

While Sullivan leaned on the gate lost in a rapture I vividly realised the truth that beauty undoubtedly lies in the eye of the beholder.

Turning back to us he voiced the thoughts roused by his contemplation.

"Do you know what it is but it would be the sport of Cork to see one of those college educated strapeens from Dublin climb over that gate and walk in to inspect that fellow. Now wouldn't it just? The class of fellow they have nowadays who couldn't tell the difference between a nanny goat and a buck rabbit unless he had the book of instructions in his hand."

After a moment's further contemplation of such a situation we continued down the boreen, where, a little further, we arrived at another gate and over it feasted our eyes on the fearsome prospect of three even more ferocious looking bulls.

"There they are. My darlings. My pride and my joy. And those are what the people up in Dublin are tricking and contriving to rob from me. And if they were to succeed, it would be far worse than death to me for what would a Sullivan be without a bull, I ask you? And how could I face all the Sullivans who went before me if I let them down. My father and his father before him and his father again all down the line kept a bull. We are written down in the graveyard and in history as the Sullivans of the Bull. But they won't succeed. Together we bate the Spaniards and together we'll bate any government."

We reached the foreshore. Professor Bolton started to unroll his ordnance map.

"Put your papers away and open your ears and listen to the true story of the battle of Kinsale as I heard it from my great-grandfather who heard it, word for word, from his great-grandfather who lived at that time."

"It was in this exact spot that the Spaniards tried to land without a permission or by your leave as though the place already belonged to them. The night was dark and they made little enough noise but enough to warn us that something was happening. As they grounded on the beach the Sullivans were ready in wait for them. As soon as they put foot on shore we let them have a volley but, in the flashes of the guns we saw that we were outnumbered by hundreds and you would think that all was lost by us. Not at all. We waited till they were all ashore and then one of us opened the gates and let out the reserves. Well, there was never a scene like it in the history of the world. In the dark the Spaniards hadn't an idea of what was happening to them and they thought that maybe the divil himself was loose amongst them. The beauties had the time of their lives, tossing them back into the boats, rolling them back into the tide, bellowing like a thousand cannons.

"The battle was soon over. The Spaniards leapt back into their boats and away with them back to Spain as though the hounds of hell were at their heels. So it was that the day was won for Ireland and the country was saved by the Sullivan bulls. And, by the same token, the parish priest, Father Ryan, was over in Spain for his holidays last year and he told me when he returned that the King of Spain had his lesson well learned and ever since he has his army training every day of the week, including Sundays, in the fighting of bulls. And where will the country be if he hears that the government have robbed us of our bulls. The Spaniards will have us on a diet of frogs before we know where we are. So now you understand my attitude and my pride and my strong sense."

So it was that Professor Bolton found the missing link in his scheme and resolved the unsatisfactory explanation which history had so far offered and accepted for the Spanish defeat at Kinsale and with it the decline and fall of Spanish power in Europe. Of course his account and interpretation was much more developed than my inexpert version of the matter and I am afraid that Sullivan's bulls lost a lot of their substantiality in the historical version.

I still think that it is remiss of the publishers to ignore this final chapter in "Europa and the Bull". If they persist in their attitude I suppose that this unlearned account will prove to be the only record of the cause of a great turning point in the history of Europe.

Thotmes the Thirty-third

THE whole affair was due, of course, to my own initial weakness in yielding to Henry's insistence that we should go to Egypt instead of our usual annual visit to the Channel Isles.

Naturally, I expected that his interest in the novelty of the trip would simmer down soon after our return and he would take up his usual routines and interests. It was, however, just not so. Instead of his interest in Egypt fading it waxed and grew as the weeks passed, until, too late, I was overwhelmed by it and powerless.

It was the matter of the cat which, I see now with hindsight, should have given me my first warning of what was to develop. Up to this Henry had always disliked cats. Then, suddenly, he displayed an interest in them to the extent of installing one in the house. When I questioned his changed attitude the bland explanation I got from him was, "But, surely you know that the ancient Egyptians worshipped cats!" I just shrugged my shoulders at the *non sequitur,* failing completely to realise its significance. Anyway, I had always wanted to have a cat about the place, and I allowed the cat, ignoring the reason.

The next hint came, and again passed unheeded, when I announced my intention of waging war on the beetles in the coal shed.

"Oh! you can't think of doing that, surely!" expostulated Henry. "You must be aware of the fact that beetles were sacred to the Egyptians!"

We had been back for about two months, when, one Sunday, over the lunch table, I happened to ask Henry how he had got on with his usual Sunday morning round of golf. In the most matter of fact manner imaginable he replied, "I wasn't playing golf today. . . . I was at church."

"You were at church!" I exclaimed with a justified astonishment. "But you haven't put your foot inside a church since the day we were married."

"True, my dear. But that was due to my former blindness."

"And what great illumination have you suffered, might I ask, to change the habits and opinions of thirty years?"

"It's perfectly and simply obvious," he replied, eagerly. "I still retain my opinion about church going in the obvious sense but perhaps you don't realise that, under the form of whatever the sect may happen to be, there remains the foundation of the ancient Egyptian worship. Unknown to themselves, the worshippers, at the conclusion of all their prayers and ceremonies, call upon the Egyptian god — Amen."

"Henry, get on with your mutton before it gets cold." Beyond this I was speechless, for I realised that this was no jesting quip. Henry was totally devoid of a sense of humour. This had been said in deadly seriousness and I simply did not know how to handle it.

For thirty years I had been able to foretell and forestall every single thought of Henry's. I could set the clock by his coming and his going and I took a justified pride in what I had made of him in that time — and now this! Under my very nose, the Henry that I knew, the Henry that I had made, was vanishing into the unknown.

Before I had time to recover my ground he attacked again. For the first time in his life he attended a local football match. On his return, in somewhat apprehensive jest I asked him if this new interest could have anything to do with Egypt.

He beamed benevolently at me as though at last I had made an intelligent remark.

"Yes, my dear, but not specifically the matter of a football match. Any sporting occasion serves the same purpose. You see, they are all unconscious manifestations of the persistent power of the Egyptian religion. In their moments of excitement and exultation the unwitting crowds still, after all these centuries, call upon the Egyptian god Ra when they shout Hurrah."

The drawing room rapidly began to look like a junk shop, littered up with the Egyptian – or Birmingham – bric a brac which Henry daily amassed. You stumbled over models of the Pyramids. You barked your shins on models of the Sphinx. Statuettes of birds and dogs and cats gathered dust. Piles of books on Egypt piled up on the floor. Magazines and catalogues relating to Egypt poured through the letter box in an avalanche.

All the incidents of daily life in Birley were interpreted in terms of Egypt. All conversational roads led back to the one place – Egypt. Too late I found myself overwhelmed, carried along in a flood of absurdity which I could no longer control, for how can you grasp the absurd? What relic of will I had left vanished on the day when Henry arrived home with a mummy in a sarcophagus. "Thotmes the Thirty Second. Guaranteed Genuine. In excellent condition. Very lucky to get it at any price."

That was installed in the spare bedroom and that was the end of any possible guests. The neighbours had been regarding us with queer looks for some time past. The hope of allies dwindled away.

When I found Henry sunbathing in the nude, in the garden, in mid-October, in Birley, I made a last mild whimper of protest, well knowing the answer I could expect – that the Egyptians worshipped the sun.

With the stupidity of despair I pointed out that he wasn't an Egyptian; that we were in Birley; that there wasn't any sun; that the neighbours might have their own views on the matter – and that he might catch a chill. The rest of the arguments meant nothing, but he caught a chill.

He retired to bed. His "Daily Telegraph" lay each day unopened on the bedside table for he had started to write a book expounding the theory he had developed that physical mummification was but the outward sign of the fundamental Egyptian civilisation, the essence of which was the mummification of their beliefs throughout the future of mankind, as exemplified in such instances as "Amen" and "Hurrah".

Then the cat died. But that was not, by any means, the end of the matter. It had, naturally, to be embalmed. In anticipation of this Henry had made a thorough book study of the processes involved and had already laid in the requisite chemicals and equipment. It shows how weak I had become, that, with scarcely any resistance at all, I was pressganged into assisting at the embalming process.

By this time I was well accustomed to his frequent late homecomings from meetings of fellow Egyptologists and had even come to look upon such occasions with relief. It was a somewhat different matter, however, when late one night the phone rang and when I answered it, found Scotland Yard at the other end.

I had to get a taxi and go up to town and lay claim to Henry. The police had found him at midnight, perched on a ladder which he had propped up against Cleopatra's Needle. They were not at all impressed by the research which he claimed to be doing. In their crude, mundane view of things he had broken quite a number of laws and bye-laws and his behaviour could only be satisfactorily explained away by attributing it to the effects of drink. So drink it had to be and I was able to lead Henry home.

He got pleurisy from this escapade and I got a breathing space in which I was able to gather together the bits and pieces of myself; to recover my strength of will and lay my plans for the future. Henry was to be led back, discreetly if necessary, but firmly undoubtedly, to the paths of his former habitude. There could be no possible question about this.

When he was convalescing I decided that one night I would lay the trap of the theatre for him. He had, formerly, been always very interested in our weekly visit to the local theatre. This week there was a thriller, much to his former taste. I booked seats and, in the evening, ordered him to dress.

Of course, I expected a protest, but I was ready for it.

"But, really, you know I can't spare the time. I am so far back in my studies over this illness."

"Yes, of course I understand that, Henry, but I do think that if you give your mind a change for a few hours you will be so refreshed that you will gain far more than you lose." Under my steady eye he wilted and a moment later he yielded. It looked as though, adroitly handled, the tide might be changed.

The play was excellent. Several times I glanced at Henry and he appeared already to be almost his former self again, caught up and engrossed with the situation on the stage. Yes, the tide seemed to be on the turn.

The third Act, with the denouement, arrived. The villain of the piece would be revealed by walking across the empty stage. The whole house was tense, Henry, apparently, not least amongst us.

Then he leaned towards me, placing his hand on my knee. "Listen! Listen, carefully . . . my Egyptian theory!" he whispered.

I listened. I listened. From far away at the back of the pit came a faint voice calling "Ices! . . . Ices! . . . Ices!"

I didn't scream. My mind and resolution snapped into an inexorable decision. Henry had reached the end of his tether. He was beyond all hope of salvation.

*　　*　　*　　*　　*　　*　　*

Despite my constant chiding he always slept on his back, so, once he was asleep it was the simplest thing in the world to press the pillow over his face for a few moments. And so, without any unseemly scene was the problem of Henry settled.

Almost immediately, however, difficulties loomed up. Speaking from experience, murder is quite a simple matter. The real problem arises with the necessary subsequent disposal of the body. That, in my opinion, should always be planned first. I lay awake for a long time with this problem unsolved. Every possible means that occurred to me contained some insurmountable obstacle.

Finally, I turned to Henry in desperation, for sometimes, by the law of averages, he did produce an intelligent solution to a problem. I called him. Then I shook him but there was no response. I switched on the bedside lamp and still there wasn't a stir out of him. So engrossed had I become in the problem that I had completely forgotten that Henry was the subject of it. He lay there, motionless, just like . . . like the mummy in the drawing room. The mummy in the drawing room! The perfect solution to my worry. Why on earth had I not thought of that before?

*   *   *   *   *   *   *   *

There was the remainder of the previous day's joint and, as Henry, in this respect at least, had not to be considered, there was no need to bother about a sweet. So I had the whole day uninterrupted to devote to the matter in hand. It was now that I reaped the reward for my dumb patience over the embalming of the cat. When I at last had Henry steeping in the embalming pickle in the bath I turned my attention to Thotmes the Thirty Second and removed its swaddlings. As I had guessed, Henry had been swindled. Thotmes was merely a crude plaster figure wrapped up in bandages.

By the time that I had finished I pride myself that I had made a really good job of Henry. It was rather a pity, in a way, that he was not in a position to appreciate it.

Yet still my worries had not come to an end. Quite apart from the sarcophagus taking up so much room there was all the other clutter about the place. Having achieved so much I didn't want to spend the rest of my life in the atmosphere of Egypt. Having scotched the mainspring of it all, it seemed absurd to have to remain with the products of it.

Amongst the accumulation which Henry had amassed were magazines devoted to Egyptology. Glancing idly through a copy of one I came across a column of advertisements relating to the sale and exchange of Egyptologia. Without more ado I wrote out an advertisement for the next issue and posted it off immediately.

"Large collection of Egyptologia for sale, including genuine mummy in sarcophagus. Owner no longer interested. Going cheap."

I had scores of replies. I answered the first most promising one and a couple of days later the prospective buyer arrived. He was most impressed by the mummy. Mummies, he explained, were his speciality and he immediately recognised the genuine article in comparison with the numbers of fictitious such which were sold to the credulous.

We fixed amicably on a price and the following day he returned with a furniture van and stowed the whole lot into it. As he went off it did occur to me that I might follow the van along for a short distance. Then I decided not to do so and closed the door.

After all, that would have been a mere formality, and I had done much more for Henry in a practical way than most wives or widows do or could do. In his wildest dreams he could never have hoped that he would go down through all future ages in the company of the Ptolomies and the Pharaohs, as Thotmes the Thirty Third instead of in a commonplace grave in the local cemetery.

Silence is Golden

"DON'T be quoting proverbs at me," warned Jeremiah, with a threatening thrust of his pipe stem. "There's no sense to them."

"I wouldn't expect you to recognise sense," snapped back Snucky Sugrue.

"They contradict each other and there can't be sense in contradictions," re-asserted Jeremiah.

"Tell me one so and I'll prove that you are wrong for a wager of a pint."

"Alright, I will, Mr. Knowall." Jeremiah searched his mind for a moment. . . . " 'Silence is golden' – there's one for you, who spend the night talking."

Snucky drained his glass and loosed his imagination from its leash. "I'll educate you now, Jeremiah, out of the depths of your ignorance by telling you how a simple man raised himself from a labouring life to ease and comfort by believing in proverbs and proving that silence is golden."

"Years back, there was a man by the name of Jim Brady. He had a job in the blasting gang on a relief work for building election roads. But one day Jim didn't manage to make the getaway when the fuse was fired. He stumbled, and when we looked round from the cover, Jim was just getting back to his feet when the shot went off, and when the stones and the dust had settled, Jim was lying where he fell – dead.

We put him on a hurdle and carried him home and told the old women to prepare him for the wake. That night we waked him like a king. We had porter and whiskey by the gallon – and it was in the days when there was real whiskey in the world. We said all the good that we could remember about him and then, when we had eased our consciences, we spoke the truth about him. All the time Brady lay there without a sound. Neither the talk nor the smell of the whiskey knocked a stir out of him. Remember that, now, Jeremiah. Remember that.

The night and the company wore away until there were only three or four left, who had got into a tangle of an argument and had either to settle it or fight before they could break up. They were hard and hot at the litigation when there was a sigh from the wake table and – Brady sat up. Then, without saying a word, he got up, put his two feet on the floor and stood there, just as he was.

The company took to their heels and ran like hell out of the house with the height of fright they got. Brady turned up to the job the following morning with nothing more wrong with him than a cut on his head and the loss of his speech. The gang were in a bit of a fix. They didn't want to be advertising themselves as a class who spent money, waking a man when he wasn't dead. They asked Brady himself about it and how it felt to be dead and had he any news of heaven or hell for them. But Brady hadn't a word – yes or no. They were entitled to believe their own eyes that all through the night there hadn't been a stir out of him while the whiskey was about him in lashings. That surely was test enough. Brady must have been dead so.

Brady, then and after, said nothing, but he did a lot – and just as important – there was a lot of things he didn't do. Brady, you see, was an intelligent man who believed in proverbs and knew that actions speak louder than words.

Now all this happened about the time for the planting of the spuds. There had been a contention in the parish for years about drills and ridges and Jim Brady had always been the leader of the faction that believed in ridges. He would not hear a word in favour of drills. But when he started on his own spuds, after coming back from the dead, he straightaway planted in drills. That only made it all the more certain that he had come back from the dead and it had needed the death to convert him, for he was an obstinate class of a man. Of course, every man in the parish followed suit. You couldn't blame them for who were they to be making right and wrong with a man who had come back from the dead.

A few years before this happened there was an ould hake of a spinster woman died and in her will she left a cottage and a tidy bit of land and a good weekly wage to be given freely and entirely and for life to a man who was this and who was that and who was all that an ould hake of a spinster might fancy a man to be. But there was no man in the parish or in any parish had such qualifications, for if there ever was such a man he would never have been let out of heaven. And all that the man had to do for it all was to keep the hedge and the grass of the chapel trimmed.

The giving of the legacy was in the hands of a committee made up of the priest, the manager of the bank and Hegarty of the pub. Every man of the parish had put in his application for the job but in every man the committee found a failure somewhere and the job remained idle and the cottage with it and all the while the money was piling up in the bank. Hegarty would turn a man down because he did not drink and the priest would turn down another because he did drink. The bank manager would not agree with the politics of the man the priest favoured and so there was never any conclusion. But every year when the time came we all made application still. The legacy had become a cant in the place so that no one ever said 'Till the end of the world' but, instead, they would say, 'Till the settling of Miss Halloran's will.'

Now Brady, before he died, was ever a great man for the pint or the glass of malt, according to his humour. It was one of the things against him with a part of the committee. But from the moment he came back all that was changed. Not once did he put his foot inside Hegarty's pub. There was something miraculous about it.

It set the people wondering and those who always voted the safe way followed his example immediately. The slow-in-the-uptake ones followed suit a day or so after. For after all he must have had a good strong reason for doing what he did and the only reason could be from what he had learnt when he was dead. Soon Hegarty was almost out of his wits. There was his fine bar, stocked to the ceiling and empty of custom from opening to closing. Trade had gone to the devil – or the other way.

Hegarty went to see the priest about it but naturally got no satisfaction when all that Brady had done overnight was what the priest had been trying to do for years. He went to Brady himself about it and argued with him and cursed him. He pointed to his wife and children and the ruin staring them in the face. But Brady said never a word but just stood, looking through him, as though he was a dummy.

The next one on Jim's programme was the bank manager. In the middle of the next fair day Brady went up to the bank when it was full and at its busiest and he wrote out on a piece of paper that he wanted what bit of money he had in the bank out. The manager had to give it to him. Brady stood there on the steps of the bank, in full view of the fair, counting his money carefully before he tucked it away in his pocket. Some of them took the hint at once. Others took the night to think what it might mean. Anyway, the following day the bank was besieged by every man in the place who had a few pounds put by, wanting it out, and the manager had to give it till the safe was empty. After that the only money he had to count was the money in his own pocket and the Dublin managers were beginning to want to know what might have happened.

The following Sunday while the parish was on its way to Mass there was Jim Brady working away in his garden, in full view, with never a move out of him in the direction of the chapel. That was the only fine day we had in that week and Brady was a whole week ahead of the rest of us. It was the same the following Sunday and the holy day that came in the same week.

That set the parish thinking on a new line. After all, there was many a man with a fierce thirst on him had given up drink by Brady's example and Brady had even gone against himself in the matter of the drills and ridges. The next Sunday about half a dozen of the men of the place missed Mass. The Sunday after that a score followed. And the Sunday after that it was like the reformation with only the women of the parish in the chapel.

The priest preached a sermon on Brady when he saw the way that things were going, saying that it was all nonsense about him coming back from the dead and that they were not to believe it. That was alright in its way but it did not get over the matter of the drills and the ridges nor yet of the drink. All that the sermon did was to whip the women up so that a cival war broke out in the parish of the women against the men. There were threats and there were scoldings. The men would be left without their dinners and they would reply by leaving the women without the wages. So it went on. But Jim Brady took no notice and went his own way, saying nothing to anyone.

The time came round again for the application for Miss Halloran's legacy, and Brady, like the rest of us, put in his application as usual. The rest of us were thrown out as we always were but there was a long sitting of the committee on Jim's application, which went on all day and for half the night. At last Jim himself was sent for to appear before them.

What happened there and what was said and what was not said no one knows – for Brady said nothing about it ever after. But the result of it was that he got the legacy and the back money attached to it. When he had it all certain and in his fist he went back to the bank and banked it there together with the money he had taken out. And he went to Mass the following Sunday and the whole parish followed him in. And he went into Hegarty's and Hegarty was very pleased to see him at any time and whatever Jim asked for, when he got his speech back, which was as soon as the matter was fixed and sealed, Hegarty was in no hurry about the payment. When Christmas came he always gave Brady a half dozen of whiskey to go with the bank manager's hamper and the priest's blessing.

There's the power of silence for you, Jeremiah, and the proof that silence is golden. You owe me a pint."

"I do not," replied Jeremiah, "for it is all a damned lie and I don't believe a word of it."

"Wasn't I the witness of every detail of it? I could tell you the very place that it all happened."

"And where was that but in your own fabricating mind?"

"No – it was in the parish of Paddy M'Ginty's goat."

"And where on earth is that?"

"You are a hard man and a tight man and a scrutinising man, Jeremiah! Would you have me give you a lesson in geography as well as in wisdom for the price of one miserable pint?"

Bottles of Smoke

DREAMS, I'd be for saying, are one of the worst inventions mankind has to suffer. For the way I look at it is that the business of living is difficult enough while you're awake without being pestered with dreams when you're asleep. Fair's fair, when all is said and done and when a man has battled through the day he's at least entitled to a decent night's sleep without having more worry and trouble to tackle than perhaps he had during the day. Particularly when he wakes up and finds that, after all, it was only a bottle of smoke, without pay or reward for all his troubles.

I had a dream years ago which made me of this opinion and I'll forever remember it, hoping that I'll never have the like of it again.

I woke out of it before dawn in the morning and I was damned glad to be awake for I'd suffered a terrible fright. But even when I was awake I didn't feel myself at all so I went down to the kitchen to make the tea for myself, but when I got down I found Clancy, a hired man I had at the time, there at the fire before me.

"Hello!" said I, "what ails you that you got out of the bed so early?"

"I got up," said he, "because I had the most frightful dream. It must have been that stew we had for supper which didn't agree with me."

"Could happen so," I said, "for I, too, had a most awful night and I am damned glad to be awake and out of it. I had the worst nightmare any man could possibly have. Blow up the fire and we'll have a heat of the tea."

"The worst nightmare any man could possibly have, indeed!" repeated Clancy as he raked aside the ashes.

"Manalive, you don't know what you're talking about. Now, if you had a nightmare that was only the half of mine I would have pity for you, or for any man having it. I wouldn't be surprised if my hair hasn't turned white as the result of the fright I had the past night. It will be weeks before I get the better of it and feel myself again."

"Get busy with the bellows and less of the talk," said I to him. "Only the tea could make me feel myself again if ever I am to feel myself again."

When Clancy heard this he dropped the bellows with a clatter and swung round on me so that I thought he had gone mad. "You don't feel yourself, did you say? You don't feel yourself! By the bones of my father, tell me so what it was that you dreamt."

"What did I dream, you ask?" said I. "May the saints preserve me from ever dreaming the likes of it again. What I dreamt and what got me out of the bed so early in the morning was that I dreamt that I was you and there is no match for that in the dreaming of mankind since the beginning of the world."

"I have the match and the beating of it still," said he, picking up the bellows and blowing the coals. "I know that my case couldn't be beat in the history of the world, past or future ... for what I dreamt last night was that I was you, and that is the end of all nightmares."

I was on the point of landing him a pasht of my fist when, suddenly, the whole horror of the business came to me. I'd said that I wasn't feeling myself and it could well be that I wasn't feeling myself because I wasn't myself. Then, Clancy had said that he wasn't feeling himself. So neither of us was feeling himself and we'd both been dreaming that we were each other. Perhaps we weren't ourselves at all but each other. Or perhaps neither of us was awake but the two of us were still dreaming; perhaps we had got mixed up in the dreaming and I was Clancy dreaming that he was me and I was the other fellow there, blowing up the fire.

"Pinch me, Clancy – if you are Clancy. Wake me up. Wake me up. Let me loose!" I screeched.

But all the ungrateful, uncharitable tinker's brat did was to put down the bellows and turn round and look me full in the face. "I will not," said he. "What kind of a fool do you take me for? I'm going to do a deal of thinking before I do anything so rash as that for it's I myself want to know where I am and who I am and whether I'm awake or dreaming still before I do any kind of pinching at all, and it may be that in the end there'll be no pinching."

"But," said I, appealing to him, "'tis only a small thing that I'm asking of you – just a bit of a pinch. Remember the time when I saved you from Mick Dan's bull and the day when you fell in the river, stroke hauling the salmon, and I saved your life."

"Yerra, that was nothing at all to what you're asking now. Not without the advice of a couple of solicitors would I even consider the matter for a moment. For how am I not to know that we are still both dreaming and just a couple of dreams met here in the kitchen and your pinching notion is just a cunning trick to wake you up and leave me then with the worn out dregs of yourself for the rest of my days? I'm not that sort of a fool."

Well, after that the two of us went at it hammer and tongs with neither one getting the better of the other, for, after all, how is any man able to tell the difference between a dream and waking, and until we had a right footing on that we were arguing at sixes and sevens. The dawn came and the kettle boiled so we agreed to an armistice until we had the tea drunk at least. But there was little pleasure in that, fond as I am of the tea, for how could I be sure that it wasn't Clancy was getting the benefit of my pleasure in it after all.

The day came clear and brought me an idea. I got the bit of mirror glass and took it over to the window and had a look into it. But, damn it, that didn't help matters much.

What I saw in the glass was familiar enough but then if I was Clancy dreaming he was me he would expect to see me and not himself.

Then Clancy had an idea. "We'll hould ourselves in leash," he suggested, "till Johnny Joe comes along for his cattle in the field beyond and then we'll call him in and ask him to decide who is who."

That struck me as about the stupidest idea I had ever heard.

"How the hell do you think that he could tell who was who? He would only see two people and say that one was you and one was me. Anyways, I wouldn't abide by his judgment between B and a bull's foot, let alone a matter of life and death like this. And what if he himself is only a part of the dreaming too. We'd have the kitchen packed with dreams and each one adding to the hurly-burly, and we'll find ourselves in the papers before we know where we are."

But Clancy was for it and I was against it and in no time at all the conference became as disorderly as a council meeting and we were spending most of our time calling it to order and making no progress at all in the matter.

"It fails me," said I in the latter end, "and it would fail any man to knock sense into your head."

At that Clancy fell silent for a moment and scratched his head and I was thinking that at last I had won the day. But then he spoke up and he spoke the biggest piece of blackguarding of the whole performance.

Said he "That being the case so, it proves beyond all manner of doubt that we are still dreaming and still changed places. For if you find such difficulty in knocking sense into what I have on my shoulders – as you might say – then it must be your head, for always, before we had the trouble of last night, it was the other way round and it was I who had the greatest difficulty in knocking sense into your head, so, the head's the same, the difficulty is the same – and we are still dreaming."

I drew back to give him the mightiest pasht of a fist that any man ever gave, when at that moment I smelt the porridge burning and leapt to the fire and rescued the pot.

Dreams or no dreams, porridge is food. Declaring an armistice for the time being we got down the bowls from the dresser and set to. For a while there was no sound but the rattle and the clash of spoons and the clamping of jaws. Then, suddenly, Clancy let out an almighty shriek. "It's alright!" he screeched. "It's alright."

"Of course it is," said I, always cool in an emergency. "Why wouldn't it be alright? Didn't I make it myself. It's damned fine porridge in fact, in spite of the bit of burning."

"Arrah! I'm not alluding to the porridge at all," said he. "It's to the dreaming."

"I thought," said I, "that we had an armistice signed on that in fairness to our digestions?"

"We don't need it any longer for the battle is over and done with."

"How do you come to make that out?" I asked him then. "Weren't we only getting into our second wind on the matter when we adjourned?"

"Maybe, but no matter.... Listen. Wasn't it always you who took the sugar with porridge, while I, being the man of greater sense, took salt? It's just dawned on me that, unknownst to ourselves, that's just what we have done. If I had eaten sugar with porridge I would have been in agony, whereas I'm feeling fine and myself."

It was true for him. "Now you mention the matter in that way, I'm feeling fine and myself once again, so it must have been only an ould cod of a dream after all, thank God. I'll tell you now what we'll do, as soon as we have the breakfast finished we'll draw up a testament that we'll never have the beef stew before going to bed."

"There's a degree of wisdom in that, I'll allow, but it's an over-rash thing for any man to put his hand to. Beef stew is damned fine feeding any time of the day or night. I suggest that we add an amendment to the effect that we won't, anyways, have so much of it." And we settled for that.

That seemed at the time to be the end of the matter but often since then I have had my doubts, for what man can tell the difference between dreaming and waking and how can he be sure. Often after that time I have looked up and seen Clancy eyeing me with a sly eye and, to tell the truth, there's often been the time when I looked at him with a kind of wonderment, as to who is who and which is which.

For when you are asleep and dreaming it's as real as being awake. Perhaps in a way it's more real. The more you think about it, the less sense you can make of the whole business. Perhaps it isn't settled after all and I'm still dreaming and at any moment now I might wake up and the whole pack of ye would disappear and vanish because you are nothing else than a part of my dreaming – a pack of bottles of smoke. It could be.

Cooked Goose

IT was ever the custom in these parts, that with the coming of the idle days of the winter, the county council would put out tenders for small jobs, such as bog roads, clearing of drains and the like ... the sort of work that a man could do with a spade and pick and a horse and cart. Before the job was started the engineer would come down to inspect the applicants and to detail the work to be done.

For one such a job Matt Leary and Mick Sullivan put in. Mick Sullivan had a small bit of mountainy land and a public house, which called itself an hotel – The Angler's Rest – during the summer when a few people would stay for the fishing. Matt Leary had a bit of land too, and a hackney car besides. So there wasn't much of a difference between them in the matter of substantiality, as you might say. But, in another fashion there was a deal of difference between them. Matt was what you might call a careful, conniving class of a man, who would have everything plotted and planned ahead and never spent a shilling without the strong hope of gaining a pound in return. Mick took a much less serious view of the world and took the ball on the hop, as it came.

So it happened that on the day of the engineer's visit Mick forgot all about the matter till the last minute. By the time that he got to the station the train had come and gone. Matt and his wife, both of them dressed in their best, were in Mulligan's with the engineer, already in the second round of drinks and deep in the talk as well. Matt had brought the wife along as she had a great gift for the flattery when there was anything to be gained. She had her own reasons for coming, quite apart, knowing well that if

100

Matt was left alone with the engineer it would be all hours of the night before they would think of moving back to the meal which she had gone to a deal of trouble to prepare, as her contribution to the settling of the bargain.

Mick sized up the situation at a glance. The game was lost before it had started. Without drawing any notice to himself he slipped to the opposite end of the bar and ordered himself a pint.

"You'll have another of the same, Mr. Carty" – which was the engineer's name – said Matt. "Then my wife and I would be greatly honoured if you would care to step back and have the bite to eat with us, for I am sure that you are starved after the journey. We have a young goose roasting below in the oven, if that might be to your liking and tempt you, and the wife is a great hand at the stuffing."

"Nothing would please me better, Matt," replied Carty. "Roast goose, to my mind, is the best of all eating. You're kindness itself," added he, with a bow to Matt's wife.

As the round was being poured Mick finished his pint with the one swallow and slipped out of the bar as unnoticed as his coming, for he felt an idea hatching in his head. He got into his car and away with him. His road home passed by Matt Leary's house and there Mick stopped. He didn't bother to knock at the door, knowing well that there was no one at home. As quick as a fox he was in and out again and he came out carrying the still sizzling goose in the baking tin. Into the car with it and on to "The Anglers Rest" not yet knowing the full of the idea.

In Mulligan's the party ended. Carty and Matt and the wife got into the car. Arrived back home, Matt took the engineer into the parlour where the table was already laid with a white linen cloth and where there was a fire for once in a while and a half bottle of whiskey on the table, for once in a while also.

Meanwhile, Mrs. Matt was busying herself with the

final layout and readying. She whipped the cream for the trifle; saw that all the odds and ends were ready on the tray and then opened the oven door to see how the goose was doing. But, as they say in the old fable, the oven was bare – the fine young goose had vanished. Beyond the smell of it there wasn't a sign of it. Mrs. Matt couldn't believe her eyes, but she had to. To explain the mystery was beyond the wit of her. It would have been beyond the wit of anyone, come to that. Clever as the cat was, it couldn't have opened the oven door and whipped the goose. Half cooked as the same goose was, when she saw it last, it couldn't have taken to its wings and flown away. And Mrs. Matt, when it came to matters of fact, didn't believe in fairies.

She put her head round the parlour door where Matt and the engineer were filling up the time by emptying the bottle and crooked her finger, beckoning Matt out. Then she explained to him what she could of the position of things, which wasn't overmuch of an explanation anyway. Matt himself couldn't give much help beyond scratching his head, for whatever help that might be.

The simple fact of the matter was that the goose had gone and that, if Mrs. Matt was the smartest woman in Ireland – which she wasn't – it would have been beyond her to catch and kill and pluck and clean and stuff and cook another goose in any kind of time that a man who was hungry enough already would call a reasonable time.

The only other meat convenient to hand was eggs and how could you offer to a man to whom you had already promised roast goose a boiled egg – or even two of them, come to that?

The engineer, left alone with his appetite, decided that if it wasn't, for the moment, being satisfied with roast goose, it may as well be eased with another drop from the bottle, and he helped himself. Meanwhile the hugger mugger went on in the kitchen. Matt and his wife started to abuse each other in whispers and to do that, at the best of times,

102

is a difficult enough thing to do and made all the more difficult when neither knows what the abusing is really about.

The minutes passed. Matt and his wife got to the stage where they had almost forgotten why they had started abusing each other and were just enjoying the abusing for its own sake. Mr. Carty, in the parlour, looked at his glass and he looked at the bottle and he couldn't overcome the fact that he had been well brought up and, for decency's sake, had at least to leave a drain. No goose and now no whiskey.

That was the situation when there was the sound of a car on the road outside, followed a moment later by a knock on the door. It was Micky.

"I was just wondering, as I happened to be passing," said he, "if the two of ye and Mr. Carty would care to come up for a quick drink before ye settle down to the business of the evening?"

The invitation saved the situation, for the time being anyway, according to Matt's way of thinking. It offered action at least and any kind of action was better than thinking about impossibilities. He slipped into the parlour and handed on Mick's invitation and he had no trouble at all in getting Mr. Carty to accept. Carty had been doing his own bit of thinking and, knowing that Micky had an hotel, or the makings of such, it held as much promise of food as there seemed to be in Leary's anyway. There was the sad sight of the empty bottle adding its persuasion as well, maybe.

There was a deal of thinking went on in that small space in a very short while. Mrs. Leary did her own bit, too. She had the hope that, with a few more drinks, the engineer might have his attention diverted away from food. Besides, there was also the chance that with a few more drinks, Matt might be making a great fellow of himself and a fool of her, by talking about the vanished goose. So she, too, accepted the invitation.

The three of them bundled into Mick's car and off with the party to "The Angler's Rest". Mick wasn't mean with the slope of the bottle either, as he treated them in the bar. The bottle had been round twice before Mary Jane, Mick's wife, made an appearance and Mick introduced her to Carty.

"I've always been hearing so much about you, Mr. Carty," said she, "and I can't say how delighted I am to be meeting you at last." The same Mary Jane would have made a fortune up at the Abbey Theatre in Dublin as an actress. She wouldn't have needed any teaching. It is she who would have done the teaching.

"Good evening, Matty and good evening, Sarah," she continued. "It's seldom that you step along this way, Sarah, but I suppose that your time is well taken up with the housework and all the poultry. But now, while you are all here, won't ye all step in and have a bite with us? It will be no bother at all beyond the laying of the extra knives and forks."

Sarah had her mouth open but before she could speak, Matt pinched her arm and she closed it again. The hunger was attacking himself badly now and the prospect of boiled eggs didn't seem a suitable diet for it. Carty, who was at the stage where food in general mattered more than any particular kind of food, had no notion of arguing about the invitation.

Micky ushered them all into the hotel dining room. Mrs. Micky bustled about laying the extra places, with a quick word here and a quick word there. "Pleasant weather for the time of the year, don't you think, Mr. Carty? ... Wasn't it the terrible thing happened to Sean Driscoll, Matt? ... Will ye have many geese for the market this year, Sarah? You always had a great name for your geese."

The serving girl brought in a great dish of spuds and another of sprouts. Then a large covered serving dish. Mrs. Micky picked up the carving knife and fork. The maid lifted the cover off the dish.

"I hope that you have no objection to roast goose, Mr. Carty? I know that there are some people who find it a bit rich."

"None at all, Ma'am," replied Carty, grabbing his knife and fork as though preparing to stab it down to the table, should it show any signs of vanishing.

"No need to ask you, Sarah and Matt, though I suppose there are times when you get a bit sick of goose."

Sarah opened her mouth again but, before she could utter either a gasp or a word, Matt had her kicked under the cover of the table. Any notions that Sarah may have had were silenced.

They were all served and they were all hungry and all speculations were lost in the serious business of eating, for, after all, roast goose is roast goose, no matter when or where or whose.

"Everything to your liking, Mr. Carty?" inquired Mrs. Micky, when the jaws were beginning to tire.

"Delicious, Mrs. Sullivan. Never tasted a finer goose in all my born days. And the stuffing is the best I ever ate."

"Nice of you to say that, Mr. Carty, though I am not really entitled to the credit for it. It's a recipe my mother gave me." Then, turning to Sarah, "I must write it down for you sometime, Sarah. I'm sure that you would like to have it."

It was Mick got the contract. Why wouldn't he? The best judgment of a man is deeds, not words. Roast goose on the plate before you, not a lot of fine talk about roast goose.

The Learys and the Sullivans have never alluded to the matter in any way at all. Why should they, for what gain could there be to anyone . . . and what loss? Nor did Sarah ever think of reminding Mary Jane about the recipe for the stuffing.

Hennigan and Finnegan

"WISHA! Wisha! Wisha!" Snucky mocked. "Yerra, Jeremiah, you're like an ould woman, with your wishing every hour of the day. Have sense man, or one of these days you'll meet a leprechaun and you'll be landed like Hennigan and Finnegan."

"Hennigan and Finnegan? Who were they?" asked Jeremiah with suspicion.

Snucky took a deep draught from his glass. "Hennigan and Finnegan? They were of the same contrary breed as yourself. The people who print the 'senseless' papers would put them down as small farmers, but that wasn't their occupation at all. The real occupation of Finnegan was hating the sight of Hennigan and Hennigan's full time job was hating the very thought of Finnegan. What they hated each other about was the last thing either of them would know – they were so occupied with the business. Maybe it was a family heirloom, inherited from their grandfathers. Anyway, that was how the land lay between them and few men ever did so hard a day's work as these two did in hating each other.

"If they went to the fair Hennigan would take his stand at one end of the town and Finnegan would be just as far out at the other end. If they had a drink 'twould be in pubs on opposite sides of the road.

"Happen one day they were both at the fair and the fair ended. Hennigan took his way home by the long easy way by road. Finnegan, knowing more about the comings and goings of Hennigan than Hennigan himself, took the short way, over the mountain. Both of them were hoping that the other had made a bad day of it. Such a thought was as natural as breathing to them.

"The night came down and Hennigan heard a sound ahead of him. He listened. It wasn't a sound made by a sheep or a bird, or any such thing. It was just 'Tap, tap, tap', and that, Hennigan knew, could mean only the one thing.

"He moved onto the grass verge and stole on like a cat till he was on top of the sound. Then he made a grab in the dark and his hand fixed on the shoulder of a jacket.

" 'Hand me over the crock of gold,' said Hennigan, 'and don't be trying any of that ould nonsense about beautiful women for I'm not interested in beautiful women – and anyway, it's dark.'

" 'Let me go,' screeched the leprechaun – for 'twas a leprechaun alright. 'I've to get back to the supper or I'll be beat.'

" 'Supper or no supper, you'll be beat unless you hand me over the crock of gold.'

" 'I've no crock of gold,' said the leprechaun, 'you've been listening to those old human rigmaroles of stories about leprechauns. There's no such thing as a crock of gold. 'Tis all an invention.'

" 'I don't know about that,' said Hennigan. 'All that I do know is that I am not letting you out of my hoult till I get the crock of gold.'

"So they went at it, hammer and tongs. The leprechaun wriggling and twisting and Hennigan struggling and wrestling to keep his hould.

" ''Tis the chance of a lifetime and I'm not going to let it pass,' said Hennigan.

" 'Have you any commonsense at all,' yelled the leprechaun in the midst of the battle, 'to think that if I had a crock of gold I'd be sitting at the side of a mountainy road on a night like this, mending a pair of shoes that aren't worth the sole leather?'

" 'I suppose that there's something in what you say after all,' answered Hennigan between the gasps. 'But still, you must have something or other or why would you be a leprechaun at all?"

" 'The only thing we have,' said the leprechaun, during an interval, 'is the power to grant a wish.'

" 'Yerra,' said Hennigan then, 'why didn't you say that at the beginning and it would have saved the two of us a deal of energy. That will do me alright.'

" 'You can have that,' answered the leprechaun, 'with a heart and a half, if only you'll let go of my ear. But I must tell you that we've been having a deal of trouble with the granting of wishes to humans lately and we've had to pass an act of parliament making a special condition on all such wishes granted.'

" 'And what might that be?' asked Hennigan.

" ''Tis simple enough. You see, we found that when we granted wishes to humans they hadn't the right way of going about the business properly and in the end, if you've any knowledge of history at all, you'll see that they always managed to do themselves more harm than good – apart from upsetting the law and order of the universe. So now, every wish we grant gives just double as much of whatever it is to the wisher's worst enemy. 'Tis a sort of insurance policy against rash wishing.'

" 'You mean now,' said Hennigan, 'cutting out the acts of parliament and insurance policies, that if I was to wish for a crock of gold I'd get it for certain?'

" 'Guaranteed and warranted – the moment you wish for it,' answered the leprechaun, 'but at the very selfsame instant your worst enemy would get two crocks of gold.'

" 'Yerra, that's not fair at all,' replied Hennigan.

" ''Tisn't for you to say whether it's fair or not. There's no one forcing you to wish. Those are the conditions laid down and signed and sealed and there's no way out of them. Now, are you taking the wish or are you not, for I'm late enough and I'm getting nothing out of this bargaining except a cold.'

" 'I'll take it,' said Hennigan. ' 'Twas ever said that you should not look a gift horse in the mouth and I'd believe that I'm a clever enough man to get the best of that class of a bargain. It just needs a bit of thinking out.'

" 'Well, the moment that you let go of me, you'll have the power of the wish on you then,' said the leprechaun.

"The moment that Hennigan let go of the leprechaun's ear he scuttled up over the mountain like a hare and was lost in the darkness. Hennigan went on his way.

"But the leprechaun didn't travel far before he hit something soft with his head in the height of his hurry in the dark. And what he hit was Finnegan's stomach. Finnegan let a screech out of him and fell on top of him so that the leprechaun could not get up and started to bawl. 'Oh!' said Finnegan, 'I thought that you were a ram or a goat but the only thing that you could be of this size and at this place and this time is a leprechaun.'

"Then the same old 'me-aw' about a crock of gold started again until at last Finnegan and the leprechaun parted on the same terms as Hennigan and the leprechaun had parted.

"Hennigan and Finnegan arrived home. They had the tea and then the two of them, in their houses on opposite sides of the stream, drew their chairs up to the fire. The two of them started the same thought. The two of them racked their brains as to how they could beat the insurance policy and each do himself the most good and the other the most harm.

"They both went to bed, with the same problem unsolved. Ever unknown to the other, each lay awake for the best part of the night, tossing and turning. The following day and the day after that and the week after that and the month and the year after that they scratched their heads with the problem unsolved.

"They talked to themselves, they neglected their food, their cattle, their crops until what little each of them had was gone from them. They got to the state where they dared not wish for even the simplest thing, like a fine day, for fear of the greater prosperity, even in this little thing,

109

of the other fellow. They had to act as watchdogs to their own thoughts and tongues lest, in carelessness, they might express a wish. They were prisoners of their own manufactured hatred and were mad with it.

"Then one day Hennigan took himself up the mountain again and he searched and searched until he found the leprechaun again.

"'Well, did you have your wish?' asked the small fellow.

"'I did not,' answered Hennigan, 'and it's about that that I have come to see you. I'd be as well off or maybe better if I was rid of the wish entirely. I was wondering maybe could I unwish it?'

"'That seems to me to be a queer way and a long way round and a terrible waste of time to get to where you were before – but then I could never understand the way in which humans go mad.'

"'It's a straight answer I'm looking for,' said Hennigan then.

"'But it's a twisted question, you must allow,' replied the leprechaun. 'I'd say that such a thing could not be done without a special act of parliament. You see, the position is that if you wish to unwish a wish then your worst enemy must unwish two wishes. That's in the contract. But how can he do that if he has ne'er a wish at all. It's no more possible than that he could untie two knots in a piece of cord which he hasn't got. Yes, 'tis a knotty problem, whichever way you look at it. However, I'll make a note of your name and put it before the next committee.'

"'Hennigan's the name.'

"'Well, that will be easy to remember anyway for I've a note made already, for another fellow by the name of Finnegan had me bothered only yesterday with the same problem.'

"'Finnegan? Finnegan did you say?' yelled Hennigan. 'A low sized ugly block of a divil?'

" 'That would about describe him,' answered the leprechaun. 'He'd a certain resemblance to yourself.'

" 'Do you mean to tell me,' roared Hennigan, 'that he's got one of your ould curses of wishes too?'

" 'Yerra, manalive, they cost us nothing,' replied the leprechaun, 'we give them, right, left and centre, to any ould fool of a human who's mad enough to want one. And, by the same token, would you be from the townland of Larrabeg?'

" 'I am,' said Hennigan. ' 'Tis Finnegan and I share it.'

" 'Then you're like peas out of the same pod. You've both got wishes and you have the same bad thoughts about each other except that Finnegan maybe has the greater share of sense between ye?'

" 'How could that be?' asked Hennigan. 'The man was born without a splink of sense.'

" ' 'Twas the other day it dawned in him when I told him how I'd given a fellow of the same cut as himself a wish and he was having the same trouble as himself with it. He guessed that it would be yourself and that was good news to him. 'Tis a miracle the way humans are able to make good of evil and evil of good.'

"Hennigan scratched his head. 'I don't see the sense to that at all.'

" 'Wasn't the power of the wish the greatest misfortune ever happened to you a couple of minutes ago? Weren't you asking me to get rid of it for you?' asked the leprechaun.

" 'I was,' replied Hennigan.

" 'Well so, when your neighbour Finnegan knew that you were in the same boat as himself he took a much better view of the situation, as humans see things. He knew that there was no greater misfortune that he could draw on you than the great fortune you thought of drawing on yourself and he went away satisfied.'

" 'There's sense to that alright,' agreed Hennigan after pondering over the matter for a while.

" 'There's what you humans call sense – though from the really sensible point of view 'tis all upside down. I've no more patience with you and I've a pair of shoes I must have done before we close for the half day. You'd best stew in your own juice.' And with that, the leprechaun scuttled off.

"Hennigan and Finnegan lived to be old men, kept alive by the satisfaction of knowing the other's misfortune and ignoring their own good fortune. That's what wishes do for you, Jeremiah. Get sense before you get caught."

The Philosopher's Stones

"SPEAKING from experience," said Tim Timothy Tim, "there's a deal to be said for employing a leprechaun as a hired man about the place, though I know that there's a lot of bigoted people wouldn't give into that at all, at all.

"They are small and neatly built and so they don't take up much room round the fire at night. They are easy feeders and good milkers. They don't belong to any trade unions and they are their own doctors. They are quick to learn and they have a lot of useful tricks of their own. Along with that they have a store of stuff in their luggage the like of which the world doesn't know at all."

I had such a one by the name of Aloysius, Aloysius McCafferty Keogh, working for me years ago and, happen one day, we were out of matches between us entirely. I turned out my pockets in the hope of finding a loose one but no good. Then Aloysius turned out his and by the time he had the collection on the grass it was beginning to look like the inside of a jackdaw's nest. There was a bit of an ould wishbone, pieces of string, a penknife with half a blade left to it; three trouser buttons; six acorns; four inch nails; two cough sweets but ne'er a match. The queerest thing of all in the collection seemed to me to be some marbles, as though he was a scholar still.

"Marbles!" snorted he when I remarked about them. "Man alive! What ails you? I took you for a man of sense and learning. Those aren't marbles at all. They're philosopher's stones, as any man with a knowledge of the world would know, seeing them."

"Wisha! Of course they are," said I, looking closer. "It was because I wasn't wearing my specs that I mistook them. Very fine ones they are, too, as I see now. 'Tis many a long day since I saw such fine ones, in fact."

"Yerra, they're good enough in their way," he replied, shovelling them back, with the rest of the collection, into his pockets, "but they have got a bit dull of late years as there is so little use for them in the way the world is going. A few centuries ago you could have sold the like of them for three or four pounds apiece, and got luck money along with that if you were stiff enough."

" 'Tis a pity all the same to see them lying idle. We must give them a bit of exercise some day when we have idle time by us. They're for turning lead into gold, if my memory serves me right from my school days, aren't they?"

"That's what they were invented for in the beginning," agreed Aloysius, "but there's no 'meas' on gold nowadays. 'Tis a class of a crime to have anything to do with it nowadays. If anyone happens to dig any of it up, straightaway the government snatches it from him and buries it even deeper than it was found in order to give the next digger more of the trouble. There's an uncle of mine by marriage in America who tells me that they have so much of it buried there in a great hole that it's making the world lopsided and that's the cause of the bad weather. . . . No. There's no 'meas' on gold these days at all. Everyone is clean daft for lead for making bullets."

Come the next rainy day, when we had nothing much better to do with our time we tried the power of the stones on some ould lead piping and flashing that had been lying about the place for years. And we found that they worked quite well, once they got worked up to the business.

Some weeks later we ran out of tea and when we came to search our pockets there wasn't the price of even a couple of ounces between the two of us.

"We're sunk!" said Aloysius, overcome with despair.

"We're not," said I, for an idea had come to me. "With that ould gold out there in the yard we ought to be able to buy enough tea to be able to swim in it. Come, help me tackle the ass to the cart. Then throw some of the stuff into it and I'll go into town and trade it for tea."

No sooner said than done and away with me into the town. I called firstly into Mahaffy's who had always a great name for their blend of tea and I told the boy at the counter that I wanted some of their very best tea.

"How much would you be wanting?" he asked.

"You can give me the fair value for that," said I, throwing a lump of my gold onto the counter.

"Yerra! What codding have you," said he, after giving a bit of a glance at it. " 'Tis to Tighe the Tinker you should go with the likes of that. We don't deal in ould brass."

"Brass!" said I. " 'Tis easily known that it wasn't long since you were taken out of petticoats and breeches if you can't tell the difference between brass and the finest of gold." With that I picked up my gold and went in next door to Dillon's. But I fared the same and no better in Dllon's. From there I went to Micky Joe's and from Micky Joe's right down the street by the way of the Widow Heraty's and even to the little hucksters shop kept by the sandyhaired fellow with the cross eyes, but the divil a grain of tea could I get from any of them but only their ignorant talk about brass.

In the end I went to the bank, thinking that at least they would have a bit more knowledge of their end of the business but it was even a higher degree of ignorance that I met there.

"How many carrots is it?" said the fellow sitting behind the bars like a tame kangaroo in Duffy's circus, when I pushed a bit of my gold through to him.

"Carrots!" said I. "Do you think that it is how I am trying to feed you? Go and get your master, for you must only be an apprentice at the trade and dealing with the ha'pence still."

Off with the lad and he brought back the Manager. The

Manager took a look at my biteen of gold. Then he took a look at me over his spectacles. Then he had another look at the gold, like a thrush that had come across a worm that he wasn't expecting at all.

"Tell me, my man," said he, clearing his throat, "where did you find this or how did you come by it?"

"I didn't find it," said I, telling him the truth. "I made it."

"Made it! Made it! How on earth could you make it?"

"By the power of consanguinity, affinity and steam locomotion," said I, at the end of my patience.

"Do you know, my man," said he to this, "that the greatest banker in the world couldn't make gold?"

"I did not," said I, "but it doesn't surprise me. From what I am learning about them I'd be surprised if they could make a pot of stirabout for themselves."

He kept me there at the counter, answering foolish questions and giving me a feast of equally useless knowledge but in the meantime, unknownst to me, in a fit of jealousy, he got one of his curates to phone to the guards' barracks and he was just keeping me there until the guards arrived. . . . So, before I knew what was rightly happening, Sergeant Geary walked in and took me by the shoulder and arrested me and hauled me along and up into the court.

"Your Honour," said the sergeant, when he had me well caged in the dock, "I charge this man with being in unlawful possession of a quantity of gold according to Chapter 97, verse 36, paragraph 12 of the Act."

"Hmmph!" said the judge, shaking the last of the after-dinner snooze off him. "Is this true, prisoner at the bar? If it's true you must say 'Guilty.' If it's a damned lie you say 'Not Guilty.' Do you understand?"

"I understand well enough and the answer is that it's not gilty but the genuine article."

"No. You don't understand," he roared. "Listen again. If it's true, then it's 'guilty.' Now have you got it?"

Well, the two of us went at it then, hammer and tongs, guilty or not guilty, true or not true, with the rest of the court putting their oars in and making an even greater porridge of the matter than it was. It wasn't for me to be giving them all a spelling lesson for they had all been at school for longer than I had ever been.

"For the love of Mike, your Grace," said I in the latter end, "have it your own way, so. Guilty you want it so Gilty it is but then, in that case you haven't any case against me and you are only making a great eejit of yourself for trying me at all. I'll probably have the law on you for unlawful detention and defamation of character. Fair's fair, even in the law courts."

"That's the first time I ever heard tell of that,"said he, scratching his head. "You sound to me like a man well up in the law. Tell me, have you ever been in the court before?"

"He has, your Worship," piped up Sergeant Geary. "He was up before for driving an ass and cart without a light."

"Oho!" said the judge to this, rubbing his hands. "A confirmed criminal. A hardened criminal. An out and out blackguard, in fact. I expect that I'll be giving him about ten years hard labour when we get down to the business in hand seriously. Now, your last chance. Guilty or not guilty?"

"Genuine gold with not a trace gilty," I roared, for no man cries stinking fish.

"Produce the evidence," screeched the judge then at Geary.

"There's an ass cart full of it outside. Am I expected to bring it all in?" asked Geary.

"An ass cart!" whipped the judge, like the dart of a dragon fly. "Has he a light on it?"

"He has not," replied Geary, with a kind of a snort in the tones of his voice.

"Ten pounds and ten minutes to pay, so!" rapped the judge.

"Will you hould, your honour!" cried Geary. "You're altogether in too much of a hurry. The law's a much more leisurely business than that. What's more, I'm not going to have my name mixed up in any kind of foolishness. I've me promotion to think about. There are excruciating circumstances in this particular case which alter it entirely."

"Oh!" said the judge to this, looking very serious. "What class of articles are those?"

"It's in the middle of the day in the middle of July and even you couldn't expect a man to be wasting a good candle in such circumstances, could you? That's simple common sense."

"I suppose I couldn't, now you come to mention it," replied the judge, after considering the matter for a while, "but then I'm not so well up in the law as you. After all, I'm only a judge. But, July or August, or even September, come to that, let me tell you that I'm not having any notions of commonsense mixed up in the law so long as I'm judge in this court, young fellow me lad. Leaving out the commonsense matter, I'll dismiss him with a caution this time, on a point of law." Then, turning to me, he said, "Dismissed without a stain on your character, but don't let me catch you at it again."

I was turning on my heel to walk out of the court when the sergeant chipped in again and roared at the judge.

"The divil fire you! You can't do that. Won't you stick to the business in hand for two small minutes together. It's the matter of the gold we are trying him for, not lights on an ass and cart in bright noon. Shall I bring it in?"

"What? The ass cart?" said the judge.

"Thon amon dieul! Will I ever knock sense into your head!" screeched the sergeant, stamping his foot with the height of impatience. "The case is about the gold, if only you'd pay attention."

"The gold? ... Oh! yes. Yes, do bring it in, by all

118

means."

The sergeant went out and he came back with a good lock of the gold and threw it down on the bench before the judge.

"If that," said he, "is not solid, hundred carat gold, according to both the letter and the spirit of the act, then my name is not Mick Geary."

The judge took it up in his hand and had a good look at it. Then he took his spectacles off to have a better look at it. He bounced it on the bench. He rubbed it on his sleeve. Then he bit it. Turning to the sergeant after all this he said, "Your name is Mick Geary alright."

Turning then to me he said "Prisoner at the bar, you are charged with a hijeous and heenus crime, according to the law, but before we go any further into that, tell me, between ourselves, how did you come by this stuff? Did you get it from the fairies or have you a mine on your land?"

"I made it," said I, telling the truth.

"Made it, did you? . . . By the hokey, but you must be a damned smart fellow, so. . . . Tell me, how did you make it?"

"Listen," said I, at the end of my patience, "I'm not a school teacher, paid by the government to teach a pack of scholars the difference between B and a bull's foot. I'm a simple, honest, decent working man who came into this town to buy a grain of tea for myself and find myself now having to stand trial for my life and to listen to the height of foolishness, along with that. I haven't got the grain of tea yet and it's early closing day. I'd be greatly obliged to you if you would get on with the business, one way or other, so that I'd know where I stand."

"I'll allow that that is decently put but I'm clean daft to know how you made this stuff. It wouldn't take you more than a minute or so to tell me that, and what's a few minutes one way or the other in a court of law?"

"I've the philosopher's stones," I replied, in order to

119

cut the matter short.

"The philosopher's stones, indeed! ... Well, well, well! ... Do you tell me that?"

At that moment the clerk of the court rang the bell. "Dinner time!" he bawled. "Court adjourned!"

"What hurry's on you?" snapped the judge. "I haven't finished this case yet and, anyway, I had a late breakfast."

"Finished or not finished — the court's adjourned. I'm not getting paid for overtime and the wife has just sent one of the children up to say that the dinner's on the table and it's a baked rabbit."

"Does she bake them with a couple of rashers over the breast of them?" asked the judge.

"She does so, and stuffs them along with that."

"Oh! That being the case I wouldn't blame you. Have it your own way so and adjourn the court." Then, turning back to me, he said, "Tell me, my good man, where will you be having your dinner?"

"Dinner, me foot!" said I. "As it's probably the last chance I'll ever have on this earth I'll be having a couple of pints in Paddy Mac's, if I can borrow the price of them off him."

"Paddy Mac's, eh? Is that the pub at the corner of the square?"

"It is," said I.

"Tell me, does he serve a good pint?"

"He does. The best in town. A beady, bubbly pint with a head you could dance 'The Peeler and the Goat' on."

"You make my mouth water. I'll tell you what we'll do. I'll meet you there in ten minutes. As soon as I have washed the dust of the law off me and got out of this fancy dress and into something respectable. We could have a chat together. We might even find that we were distantly related. . . . Court adjourned, by judge's orders." With that the guards and the solicitors tore out of the court like a pack of scholars loosed from school, knocking each other over in their haste as though they must all have been having baked rabbit for dinner.

I went down to Paddy Mac's, and, decent man that he is, he loaned me the price of a couple of pints. I was only getting intimate with the first pint when, sure enough, along came the judge. Slipping into the snug beside me he said, "Finish that up and we'll have another."

When Paddy Mac had brought the fresh pints and had taken himself away, the judge got down to business. He pestered me and he moidered me so much about the stones that at last I had to show him one which I happened to have in my pocket. When he saw it he was clean mad to have it or a piece of it, like a child who has seen sweets. But I held tough, for philosopher's stones aren't two a penny. He started to soften me with another pint. Then a half one and then a ball of malt.

The clerk of the court came in and told him that the court was opened again. He told him to go back and close it again. Still I held my ground. Finally, when I had got him to swear on oath, with Paddy Mac as witness, that he would go back to the court and sponge out of the charge against me I gave in to him. I borrowed a hammer from Paddy Mac and cracked off a fair bit of the stone and gave it to him. Away with him then, as pleased as a dog with two tails.

I didn't care, however, for the inspiration of the drink had given me another idea, which would solve all my troubles. The idea which had come to me was the remembrance that when we changed the lead into gold we discovered that we had to give the lead a swipe with the stone from left to right. When we did it from right to left nothing happened. The great idea was to see what would happen when you did the opposite, starting with the gold. I'd proved to myself that there was no 'meas' on gold and it was only a trouble maker and I would be a damned sight better off with lead.

As soon as I had the drink finished I went back to where I had the ass tethered to put the idea to trial. The moment I

121

tried it it worked. Without a blink of hesitation or a false start each piece of gold turned back to lead as I stroked it with the stone. In no time at all I had everything put back into right order.

Away with me then with my load of lead to Tighe the Tinker and I had no trouble at all in striking a good bargain with him for ready cash for he was getting a fierce price for lead and buying and stealing every bit he laid eyes on. I came out of the tangle with the price of half a chest of tea and along with that I bought a barm brack for the supper and a new lid for my pipe.

The following week Johnny Joe came up with the paper and the great account there was in it of the case of assault and battery which had happened in the town.

It seemed, according to the account, that the judge, as soon as he had the bit of the philosopher's stone got, went raving round the town, with his tongue hanging out, searching for a bit of lead to try out the power of the stone. But the divil a bit of it could he find anywhere for Tighe the Tinker had it all whipped and gathered up into his yard. But the ould fellow followed the scent of it and in the end he came to ground in Tighe's yard. Tighe was out at the time. When he saw the great heap of lead gathered up there he went clean daft entirely. What did he do but changed every bit of it into gold by the power of the stone.

Tighe came back just as he was finishing the job, and seeing what he had done and thinking it was brass and knowing the poor price there was for brass compared with lead, he went for the judge, hammer and tongs, and assaulted and battered him.

Tighe was arrested and charged but there were excruciating circumstances put in and so the case wasn't finished in that edition of the paper and we never rightly heard the end of it. There were some said this and others said the opposite and we forgot all about it, but it wasn't quite the end of the stones.

Some months later Aloysius had another idea about them.

"I wonder," said he to me, "would the stones be abreast of the times and know their history lessons rightly and so know the great change that there has come into the world? Now that there's no longer any 'meas' on gold, and paper is all the fashion, would they have changed their dance according to the tune and change paper into pound notes?"

"There's nothing urgent to be done at the moment," said I, "we may as well give them an examination."

So we got a bit of an ould newspaper and we tested the stones for their knowledge of history, and it was soon to be seen that the stones knew the way things were and how the world was preferring the shadow for the substance. There, before our eyes, with one swipe of the stone, the piece of paper changed into a fine, clean one pound note, as clean as ever you could get from the bank.

We made some experiments and we discovered that there was a trick in this new trade as in all trades and the results depended on what class of paper we used. Some papers changed into genuine notes while others changed only into false counterfeit notes. For a while we couldn't tell the reason, but in Aloysius's opinion it all depended on their politics. And he could be right.